"WHEN YOU SMILE LIKE THAT, YOU'RE ENCHANTING!"

Before Leonie, her eyes widening in alarm, could pull away, Deveril crushed her to him, seeking her mouth in a bruising kiss that set her heart pounding and her blood coursing fiercely through her veins.

She was exquisitely aware of his masculine magnetism so close to her. His questing lips moved hungrily to her closed eyelids and down to her throat. Then, as his mouth closed down on hers again, Leonie shuddered and strained away from him, beating her hands against his shoulders, and when that proved ineffectual, grabbing a handful of his hair. He released her suddenly, stumbling back and breathing hard, while his face wore a curiously dazed expression.

"How dare you—how dare you force yourself on me," exclaimed Leonie, her voice shrill with outrage, and outrage even more vehement, perhaps, because she knew there had been a moment when she had been tempted to yield to the violence of Deveril's emotions...

Also by Diana Delmore

Anthea
Dorinda
Cassandra*

Published by
WARNER BOOKS

*forthcoming

ATTENTION: SCHOOLS AND CORPORATIONS

WARNER books are available at quantity discounts with bulk purchase for educational, business, or sales promotional use. For information, please write to: SPECIAL SALES DEPARTMENT, WARNER BOOKS, 666 FIFTH AVENUE, NEW YORK, N.Y. 10103.

**ARE THERE WARNER BOOKS
YOU WANT BUT CANNOT FIND IN YOUR LOCAL STORES?**

You can get any WARNER BOOKS title in print. Simply send title and retail price, plus 50¢ per order and 50¢ per copy to cover mailing and handling costs for each book desired. New York State and California residents add applicable sales tax. Enclose check or money order only, no cash please, to: WARNER BOOKS, P.O. BOX 690, NEW YORK, N.Y. 10019.

Diana Delmore

WARNER BOOKS

A Warner Communications Company

All the characters and events in this story are fictitious.

WARNER BOOKS EDITION

Copyright © 1984 by Lois S. Nollet

All rights reserved. No part of this book may be reproduced or transmitted in any form or by any means, electric or mechanical, including photocopying, recording, or by any information storage and retrieval system, without permission in writing from the Publisher.

This Warner Books edition is published by arrangement with Walker and Company, 720 Fifth Avenue, New York, N.Y. 10019

Warner Books, Inc.
666 Fifth Avenue
New York, N.Y. 10103

 A Warner Communications Company

Printed in the United States of America
First Warner Books Printing: December, 1985
10 9 8 7 6 5 4 3 2 1

1

FROM HER WINDOW seat in the library of Wanstead Abbey, Leonie watched the mourners driving away down the avenue. She observed that the rain had stopped at last and the sun was trying to fight its way through the leaden clouds that still overshadowed this day in early May which had seen the sixth Viscount Linton carried to his eternal rest.

The library door opened, and Leonie rose as Georgina, the viscount's widow and second wife, entered the room, followed by her stepson the new viscount, and the family lawyer.

"If you will all be seated, we will proceed to the reading of the last will and testament of Francis, Viscount Linton," said Mr. Esmond, clearing his throat.

"One moment, please, Mr. Esmond," said Lady Linton, her sharp tone and frowning brow at odds with her appearance of ethereal blond loveliness, set off so perfectly by the gown of black bombazine and the widow's cap with its long, floating veil. "I would like to know why Mlle. de Montbarey is present in this room. Surely she in no way figures in my husband's will."

"Forgive me for correcting you, Lady Linton, but Mlle. de Montbarey is indeed mentioned in your husband's will. That is why I asked her to be present."

"I see. Very well, then, Mr. Esmond," said Lady Linton after an icy pause. "Please begin the reading."

Her mind retreating into its own thoughts, Leonie paid little attention to Mr. Esmond's dry drone. She was aware, of course, that Lady Linton disliked her, but until today the viscountess had never displayed such overt hostility. It had been understandable two years previously that Georgina should be opposed to the appointment of a seventeen-year-old girl of French émigré parentage as governess to the Linton daughters. Leonie had had no formal schooling, having been educated at home by her father, the Baron de Montbarey, and it was clear to everyone that it was only out of kindness that she was hired when the baron's worsening heart ailment had cut short his career as a tutor. When, however, much to Lord Linton's satisfaction, it became clear that the new governess had a real flair for teaching, Leonie had hoped that Lady Linton would become, if not happy with the appointment, at least reconciled to it. Evidently this had not happened.

"To Mlle. Leonie de Montbarey I bequeath the sum of fifty pounds and my silver and ivory chess set, in memory of my friendship with her late father, Armand, Baron de Montbarey."

Leonie gasped. Fifty pounds was a vast sum, more than double her annual salary. She silently blessed the viscount. She had refused his offer of money after her father's death, knowing that Armand de Montbarey would have writhed at the thought of his daughter's accepting charity. This bequest was the viscount's way of helping her to discharge the burden of debt that had been weighing so heavily upon her. Now she could pay for her parent's modest funerals and for headstones to mark their graves, and she could at last take care of kind Dr. Turner's fees.

When Mr. Esmond had finished reading the will and had bowed himself out, Leonie approached Lady Linton. "This is my first opportunity to offer my condolences," she said quietly. "Lord Linton was a kind, generous man, and I will miss him very much. He was a wonderful friend to my father. Each time I look at that beautiful chess set, I will be reminded of the many times they played together." She turned to the new viscount, standing beside his stepmother. Robert Linton was a tall, gangling boy of seventeen, with a thin, expressive face and an air of nervous diffidence that made him seem even younger. "Robert, you've lost a good friend as well as a good father. From my own experience, I know that there will be a great void in your life for a very long time."

"Thank you, mademoiselle, you're most kind," said the viscountess with a stiff, perfunctory courtesy, while Robert flashed Leonie a shy smile that completely transformed his young face.

"I realise that you won't wish the girls to have any lessons just at this time, Lady Linton. Perhaps you could send me word when you feel that the lessons should be resumed."

The viscountess's eyes narrowed. "Actually, I would like to discuss the matter with you immediately. Robert, will you excuse us?"

After Robert had left, the viscountess indicated a chair and sat down opposite Leonie. "I had intended to speak to you a little later," she said coldly, "but I see little point in putting off what I presume will come as an unpleasant shock to you. To put it frankly, I've decided to dispense with your services."

"I see. May I ask why?" Leonie's hands were clenched tightly together in her lap, and she fought back a momentary feeling of panic at the thought of leaving Wanstead Abbey and striking out on her own.

Lady Linton lifted an eyebrow. "Come now, mademoiselle,

surely you realise that I've never considered you to be a suitable person to hold the post of governess to my daughters and to my younger sister. You were—are—much too young for such a position. You are not qualified to instruct in drawing, or water colours, or playing the harp, nor are you accomplished in such arts as embroidery, or ornamental fancy work, or netting, or painting on fans. You have never, in point of fact, actually set foot in a proper school of any kind. I think that very few people would quarrel with my poor opinion of your qualifications."

Leonie wondered how she could have failed to recognise the strength of Lady Linton's animosity. She had no real conviction that she could change the viscountess's mind, but she said composedly, "It is true that I never attended a young ladies' academy, but I feel that I acquired a very good education from my father. I have been able to instruct your daughters and your sister in French, Italian, and English literature, the proper use of the globes, and simple arithmetic, and I have taught them to play on the pianoforte. Lord Linton, in fact, seemed very well satisfied with my work."

The colour rose in the viscountess's porcelain cheeks. "My late husband was old-fashioned," she said coldly. "His mother was a famous bluestocking, with her own salon. Nowadays the only important training for a girl is to enable her to marry well. For that she need only express herself well in her own language, perhaps know a smattering of French, sing and draw a little and comport herself gracefully in society. Scholarship is quite unnecessary—even undesirable. In sum, mademoiselle, my ideal candidate for the post of governess would be a mature gentlewoman from a good *English* family, accomplished in those graceful little arts that give a lady such distinction."

"You need not go on, Lady Linton," said Leonie. "I will be

happy to leave as soon as you have found a suitable replacement."

"As a matter of fact, I already have someone in mind. I should prefer that you leave immediately. I had planned to give you half a year's salary, but in view of my late husband's very generous bequest to you"—Lady Linton's voice dripped with acid—"that will be unnecessary. Also, I would like you to vacate, within a week's time, the cottage you have been occupying on the estate."

Leonie looked up in surprise. "Leave the cottage immediately? But I understood..."

The viscountess's lip curled unpleasantly. "Surely you did not think that you could live in the cottage permanently, mademoiselle? We are all aware that my husband offered the use of this very comfortable property as a kindness to your father when he became tutor to my stepson some six years ago. With an ailing wife and a young daughter, it would have been a hardship for him to be a resident tutor. Even after your father became unable to work, and my stepson went off to Harrow, my husband allowed your family to stay on—I well remember the viscount saying to me, 'My dear, we cannot allow this man to go to the poorhouse.' And that, of course, is when you were offered the post as governess. Now that you will no longer be filling that position, I really see no reason why I should continue to allow you to live on the estate. More specifically, I'm aware that my daughters and my sister are fond of you and will feel a schoolgirlish grief when you leave. It will be much better for them if you make a clean break and leave the area altogether, rather than have your continued occupancy of the cottage to be a constant reminder to them of your presence. Incidentally, you will be glad to know that I am prepared to give you a letter of reference; I assure you that I will make it as enthusiastic as I conscientiously can."

As the viscountess spoke, Leonie quivered with rage. Her quick temper had always been a problem, even though her proud father had repeatedly told her, "People in our position cannot afford anger, *ma fille*." But Lady Linton's venomous implication that only the viscount's generosity had saved her parents from the poorhouse touched Leonie on the raw, as did the suggestion that she had so little pride that she would have attempted to go on living in the estate cottage after she no longer had any connection with the Linton family. She breathed deeply, struggling to rein in her anger, but the expression of malicious pleasure on Lady Linton's face was the final straw.

"You have every right to dispossess me, Lady Linton, and I will leave the cottage well within your time limit," Leonie burst out, "but please don't think me so stupid that I don't know your real reason for wanting me off the premises. Your concern isn't for your daughters' tender feelings at all; what you really fear is the possibility that I might ensnare your stepson's affections."

Lady Linton's eyes flashed. "I had hoped to sever our connections with you with some degree of civility," she exclaimed angrily, "but you make that impossible. Yes, you're quite right about my fears. Will you deny that you have been preying on my stepson's callow sensibilities ever since your arrival in this house?"

"Certainly I deny it. Robert is only seventeen years of age. He may have—I believe he has—formed some sort of romantic schoolboy attachment to me, but I assure you, I have never encouraged him in the slightest."

"You would, naturally, attempt to conceal your scheming."

"Lady Linton, there has been no scheming. Even if Robert were a few years older, even if I cared for him, the match would still be unsuitable. I have no dowry, and scandal would inevitably attach to the fact that I have been an employee in this house."

"You state my own case against you so disarmingly that I am almost tempted to believe you," said the viscountess. "Almost, but not quite. I've never underestimated your intelligence, mademoiselle."

"Nor my lineage, either," flashed Leonie. "If Robert were to marry me, it would not be such a bad match—my family traces its line back to the court of Charlemagne. Much farther back than the bride you have in mind for Robert." She smiled tauntingly. "*You* will scarcely deny, Lady Linton, that you brought your sister Flora to live with you in the hope that one day she and Robert would marry." Almost before the words were out of her mouth she wished that she could reclaim them.

"Leave this house immediately. And vacate your cottage in a week's time or I'll send my baliff to evict you," spluttered Lady Linton, almost incoherent with rage.

Leonie left the library without a word or another glance at Lady Linton. Her back was still rigid with outraged pride, but reason was beginning to overcome her feelings, and she thought ruefully that she could scarcely have hit upon a better way to scuttle her future if she had made a deliberate effort. She could almost hear her father's aloof voice saying that Lady Linton had made a very advantageous marriage indeed, considering that her father had been an impoverished country squire from the wilds of Yorkshire. Thin-skinned about her unimpressive family background and anxious to arrange a good marriage for one of her sisters—and doubtless to ensure a hold on Robert's property and fortune even after he achieved his majority—the viscountess would never forgive her governess's imprudent accusation. Leonie realized that it would now be useless to expect any kind of recommendation or character reference from her.

As she stepped into the entrance hall, Robert Linton materialised from the door of the drawing room, where

Leonie was sure he had been lying in wait for her. "Oh, there you are, mademoiselle," he said in a tone of bright discovery. "I was hoping to see you again this morning. Are you going to the cottage? May I walk along with you?"

Leonie sighed. She did not feel that she could cope just at this time with Robert's adolescent gallantries. "No, Robert, I don't think that would be very wise."

"Not wise? What do you mean? I wanted to thank you for your kind expression of sympathy, and I thought we might talk, too, just a bit, about my future..."

"I don't really have any time to talk with you, Robert. You see, Lady Linton has just dismissed me from my post. I must pack up the cottage and leave the estate within the week."

"Dismissed you? But why?" Robert paused, setting his jaw. "I know why, I suppose. Mama is always saying that you don't teach the girls netting, or painting on fans, or any of that foolishness. Mademoiselle, let me speak to her. Now that I'm—well, I *am* the head of the family now, I should have some say about my sisters' education..."

Leonie looked up into the boy's anxious, vulnerable young face, suppressing an affectionate wish to spare his feelings. Better, as his stepmother had suggested, to make a clean break. "It wouldn't be of any use to speak to Lady Linton," she said gently. "She disapproves of your—friendship—with me. In fact, her principal reason for dismissing me is to break up that friendship."

Bright colour flooded Robert's face and Leonie looked tactfully away. Doubtless Robert had deceived himself into believing that his feelings for Leonie were hidden both from the object of his love and from his family. After a moment she turned back to him. "I think it would be best if I didn't see you again, Robert. Or your sisters and Flora, either. Will you say good-bye to them for me? Tell them that I will always remember them, and ask them to study hard for their new governess." She held out her hand. "Good-bye. Thank you for all your kindnesses to me since I first came to Wanstead Abbey."

Seizing her hand, Robert stammered, "Mademoiselle, I can't let you leave us like this. You've no family now, no friends..."

Pulling back her hand, Leonie said firmly, "Thank you for your concern, but I can manage very well." She stepped back, curtseying formally, as a conventional mask dropped over her expression. "Good-bye, Lord Linton."

As she walked the scant mile to her cottage in the village, Leonie hugged her pelisse around herself against the cold, damp late-afternoon air, and felt grateful that she had remembered to don her pattens—shoes with wooden soles raised on metal rings, intended to be worn in muddy weather. Walking briskly, she soon reached the cottage, easily the most substantial structure in the village, a solid stone building with a thatched roof and glazed casements. The front entrance opened directly into a kitchen with flagged floor and large stone fireplace, simple but sturdy oaken furniture and neat shelves for pewter and stoneware vessels, cheese, herbs and other condiments. Behind the kitchen was a small parlour, and a flight of short, steep stairs led to two bedrooms above.

Leonie stirred the banked logs in the fireplace and swung a kettle on the crane over the flames. Dipping a brimstone-tipped match into the fire, she lit the rushlight in its iron holder on the table. She slipped off her pelisse and bonnet, hung them neatly over pegs on the wall and sat down rather wearily in her father's wooden armchair before the fire, waiting for the kettle to boil. She gazed around the neatly kept kitchen, remembering how much her parents had enjoyed the spaciousness and comfort of the cottage after so many years of cramped and inadequate quarters. But, Leonie thought, as she poured herself a cup of tea and returned to the armchair, even the comparative comfort of this cottage must have seemed pitifully Spartan to her parents on those occasions— rare in recent years—when they allowed themselves to reflect on their lost lives in France before the revolution. During her childhood they had often spoken to her of those early years, but with the accession of Napoleon, and especially after he became emperor, they had come to realise that they would probably never return to France and had ceased to speak of the past.

Armand de Montbarey came from an old, titled and prosperous family with extensive estates in Champagne. He had served in the Musketeers in his youth, but after his marriage he had settled down on his estates. His marriage was a love match, and he and his wife Annette, both of them scholarly and musical in their tastes, chose country living over court life at Versailles. But, much as they preferred their simple and retired life style, they were both aristocrats who thought of king and country as one. After the onset of the revolution and the failure of the royal family's attempt to escape from France, Armand de Montbarey had felt it was his duty to go with Annette to Coblentz and to join the Army of the Princes under Condé, knowing that the move would automatically result in the confiscation of all the property he had left behind. With the defeat of Condé at Valmy in 1792, the Montbareys had no choice but to join the mob of titled refugees fleeing to the Low Countries ahead of the victorious revolutionary armies.

In Holland, after waiting for weeks in a crowded boarding house, fearful for the health of their sickly baby, their money almost gone, the Montbareys finally obtained passage in the hold of a merchant ship. Leonie herself had no memory of the passage, but she could recall her parents' tales of their days of discomfort in tiny, straw-filled stalls just over two feet wide, separated from their fellow refugees by partitions one foot high. Once arrived in England, their resources reduced to a few remaining pieces of Annette's jewellry, they stayed briefly in London, then decided to move to a rural area near Winchester, where it was believed that the air and the climate would be better for Leonie's health.

Like his fellow émigrés, most of whom had never worked a day in their lives, Armand de Montbarey had to find a way to support his family. He was more fortunate than most, for he spoke fluent English, and with his scholarly background he soon began giving lessons in French, Italian, Latin, mathematics and even fencing to the sons of prosperous tradesmen in the area. Annette took pupils on the pianoforte. With careful management they achieved a kind of meagre comfort. But then, some six years before, Annette discovered the first symptoms of consumption, and Armand was glad to accept the position of tutor to the son of Viscount Linton, with whom he formed a fast friendship, playing interminable games of chess and having long discussions on art and music. After the lingering death of his wife, Armand himself fell ill—the doctor told Leonie that it was a heart ailment, but she had always believed that grief contributed to his illness—and it was then that Viscount Linton had offered Leonie the post of governess to his daughters and to his young sister-in-law.

Leonie sighed. She, too, had come to love the cottage, and she would always look back on her years there, despite the death of her parents, as a time of peace and happiness. But now, she thought, knitting her brow, she must not only leave the cottage, she must make plans for the future, a future that seemed very uncertain and rather frighteningly lonely. Would it be possible, she wondered, to vacate the cottage but stay on in the village? Thanks to the viscount's bequest, she had enough money to settle her debts and to support herself for a year or more. She had a number of friendly acquaintances in the place—kindly Dr. Turner, the vicar and his family. Perhaps she might give lessons on the pianoforte, as her mother had done before her, though she could think of few potential students. Or perhaps there would be an opening in the dame school operated by Miss Ponsonby. Almost immediately, Leonie shook her head against such dreaming. Lady Linton would consider Leonie's residence in the village just as undesirable as her occupancy of the cottage. The viscountess's poisonous tongue and undeniable influence in village concerns would soon make Leonie's position there untenable.

But if not the village, where? Winchester, where she and her parents had lived for some years? No, Winchester was too provincial, too close, also, to Wanstead Abbey and the long arm of Lady Linton.

She would, thought Leonie suddenly, go to London. There in the great metropolis, surely, she would be able to find some form of employment: she could give lessons in French or Italian, or on the pianoforte, or obtain a position in a school or even another post as governess, despite her lack of references from Lady Linton. Perhaps, also, she might contact one or more of her father's émigré friends who had stayed on in London; Armand de Montbarey had corresponded with these friends for a period after he had settled in Winchester, and though the letters had dwindled away to nothing in recent years, some of these old acquaintances might still be living in London and be willing to extend a helping hand.

Rising, Leonie walked resolutely into the parlour. She would begin packing up her belongings immediately and leave the cottage well before the viscountess's deadline. In the main, she need concern herself only with personal possessions, since most of the furnishings of the cottage belonged to the estate. As she entered the parlour she paused, looking wistfully at her mother's pianoforte. The vicar, she was sure, would be glad to house the instrument for her temporarily. Moving about the room, she picked up a small cloisonné clock, an enamelled snuffbox, an armful of her father's precious books, and took them over to the old carved chest that contained most of the cherished mementos from the elder Montbarey's past. Leonie had not been able to bring herself to examine the contents of the chest in the months that had elapsed since her father's death, but now she knelt down on the floor and lifted the lid.

Catching her breath, she reached out for a small object wrapped in silk, in the folds of which was tucked an envelope bearing her name in her father's cramped handwriting. She held the parcel, turning it over and over between her hands, while her fingers absently caressed the silk and her eyes brimmed with tears. Then she placed the parcel beside her on the floor; somehow, she dreaded to read her father's last message, written, as it must have been, when he was old, and in pain and dying, and apprehensive about his daughter's future. She would read the letter later, after she completed the packing.

The chest contained an unlikely assortment of oddments, as she discovered when she began to empty it, trying to decide if any of the items should be disposed of. There was a packet of letters from her father's émigré friends in London; these she set aside to peruse later for addresses. A shallow box held a number of papers: the deeds to the family property in Champagne—useless now, as the house and lands had been confiscated many years before; some yellowing and crumbling newspaper clippings recounting the deaths on the guillotine of King Louis XVI and his queen; letters written by her parents to each other—not many because they had seldom been parted; and copies of their baptismal and marriage certificates. Another box contained a few pieces of inexpensive jewellry—some cameos, a bracelet set with carnelians, a coral necklace. Her mother's good jewellry had gone years before, of course, to pay for their expenses in Coblentz, their passage to England and the purchase of the pianoforte. Then there were the articles of clothing, all quaintly out of date, saved, Leonie guessed, because they represented a tie to the past: her father's green uniform of the *Guet des Gardes*, reversed with scarlet and laced with silver; several of her mother's dresses, with their elaborate puffed overskirts and embroidered satin petticoats; a "suit of knots," a set of gaily colored ribbon bows; and a "cardinal," a hooded cloak lined with opulent red satin and edged with ermine. And finally, at the bottom of the box, the family Bible; she leafed through the pages listing births, deaths and marriages, noting the birth, so many years ago in a different age, of Armand de Montbarey in 1755, and his marriage to Annette de Rivière in 1780. Her parents had waited ten years for the birth of their only child, Leonie thought, and then paused with a puzzled frown: her meticulous father had unaccountably neglected to record her own birth. She continued to stare down at the Bible for a few moments, then shook her head and started to repack the chest. She could not bring herself to dispose of any of its contents; perhaps the vicar would keep both the chest and the pianoforte for her.

Taking the box of jewellry, the packet of letters from her father's émigré friends and the silk-wrapped parcel, Leonie returned to the kitchen and sat down again in the armchair beside the fire. She reached out to poke at the coals, poured herself a cup of now cold tea, and finally, with an inexplicable sense of reluctance, almost of disquietude, she opened her father's letter.

"My dearest Leonie," the letter began,

"I am a selfish man and not a very brave one, as you will discover when you read this letter. But I have loved you all your life as tenderly as any father could. I offer those paternal feelings as my only excuse, and I hope that you will find it in your heart to forgive me for withholding from you the facts of your real parentage.

"My darling little girl, you are my daughter only by adoption. Your mother and I pretended for years that you were born to us—in fact, your mother begged me to the end of her life not to tell you the truth—but I have always known that you have the right to that truth. The right to know it from me, rather than to have it blurted out to you by some stranger. You see, we left London and our many friends there, most of whom knew about your adoption, not primarily because of your health as we had always told you, but to rear you among people who knew nothing of your background, who could never reveal to you, even inadvertently, the fact that you were not our natural daughter.

"You came into our lives at Rotterdam, late in 1792. Annette and I were living in a boarding house, waiting for the weathercock to turn north so that we could board ship for England. We heard about a young woman in the house, also a lodger, who was dying of fever. Mme. de Mirecourt was already in a delirium when we came to her to offer any assistance that we could, and she died without recovering consciousness, leaving behind her a sickly, delicate little girl, by our estimate about two years old. Other occupants of the house who knew the woman said that she was already ill when she arrived in Rotterdam and that she had never revealed any details about herself. But in her delirium she spoke with grief of her husband—she called him Leonard—and we conjectured that he may have fought and died with Condé's Army of the Princes. We assumed that she was a gentlewoman—her French, even in her delirium, was cultivated and correct, and her clothes, though worn and travel-stained, were originally of good quality, as was the pearl cross she wore around her neck.

"The young woman was practically penniless when she

died; the few francs in her possession were not enough to buy her passage to England, if it had been her intention to go there. We speculated that she might have intended to sell her pearl cross and two miniatures, her only possessions of any value. Nor did she leave behind any papers that might have given us some information about her identity—among her fellow lodgers she was known simply as Mme. de Mirecourt. Sad to say, not one person knew the Christian name of the child.

"What, then, was to be done? Those of us who could afford even the tiniest contribution helped to arrange a simple burial for the mother, but there was the child. The only real sorrow in our marriage, mine and Annette's, was our failure to become parents. Annette suggested that we take the baby—you—with us to London, where, among the large numbers of French émigrés, we might find someone who recognised your mother's name or the pictures in the miniatures. We named you Leonie, after your father. I think I knew from the beginning that Annette would never willingly give you up, that she wanted to rear you as the child she never had. In a very little while I completely shared her sentiments. We made little effort, frankly, to circulate your story in émigré circles, and within a few months we left London to settle near Winchester.

"In the parcel that accompanies this letter I have enclosed your only inheritance from your natural mother. As you will see when you examine the miniatures, the pearl cross is identical to the one worn by the young girl in the portrait, which is, we were sure, a likeness of your mother before illness and grief took their toll. She is wearing a dress in the "Creole" style made so popular by our late queen; Annette speculated from this that she might have been presented at Versailles, but of course that is pure conjecture. The other portrait is almost surely that of your father, from his dress and bearing a man of obvious consequence.

"So there it is, *ma fille:* let me have the joy of calling you that one last time. For you really were our daughter, Leonie, in every way that counts. Au revoir, ma chère; think of your mother and me sometimes, and remember that you had all our love."

As she put down the letter, Leonie was in a state of numbed shock. As if in a daze, she mechanically unwrapped the silken parcel and took out the pearl cross and the two miniatures, or, rather, small half-figure paintings, in oval gold frames edged with tiny diamonds. The frames themselves were the work of a skilled artisan and were probably very valuable; the paintings showed the same high degree of artistic skill.

The girl in the miniature was very young, about seventeen or eighteen years of age, with large brown eyes set in a delicate oval face; she was wearing a simple white gauze dress with wide ruffles at the round neckline, long full sleeves caught in puffs and a knot of white ribbon at the breast. Around her slim neck was a black velvet ribbon, that held the pearl cross. On her powdered hair, dressed in elaborate wide curls, the girl wore a large, wide-brimmed straw hat, dipping low on one side and trimmed with a bunch of flowers.

Despite the great contrast between the dress styles and hair arrangements of a generation ago and those of 1809, Leonie was conscious of a haunting sense of familiarity as she gazed at the pictured face. It was several minutes before she realised that she was looking at a replica of herself. The girl in the portrait had powdered hair, but Leonie guessed that her unknown mother's porcelain and wild rose complexion had been crowned, like her own, by a wealth of reddish-gold hair.

The man portrayed in the other miniature seemed considerably older. He appeared to be in his early thirties, with strong features and penetrating blue eyes. His hair, like his wife's—if she was his wife—was powdered, arranged with small side curls and a queue, and he wore a gold-laced blue velvet coat with an embroidered waistcoat.

Leonie stared down at the paintings for long moments, unable to comprehend that the identity which she had always assumed to be hers had ceased to exist. She was not a member of the Montbarey family in their long line stretching back to the Carolingian court, but the daughter of these handsome strangers.

Suddenly she burst into tears, unable to bear this added blow after the long strain of mourning for her father and today's unexpected exile from Wanstead Abbey at the hands of Lady Linton.

"Mademoiselle, what's wrong? Please, if there's anything I can do to help..."

Startled, Leonie looked up into the worried young face of Robert Linton. She swallowed hard, drawing away from his comforting arm and reaching for a handkerchief. Soon she was composed enough to say, "I didn't hear you come in, Robert—and I was having a silly, sentimental cry. Nothing serious at all, I assure you. But what are you doing here? I thought that we had agreed..."

Robert set his jaw. "I know you said we shouldn't meet again, but I've thought about it, and I refuse to allow my stepmother's spite to destroy our friendship."

"Lady Linton is your legal guardian, Robert," Leonie reminded him.

"Yes, but she has no right to choose my friends for me. She can't stop me from seeing you occasionally, now, before I return to Harrow, and during the summer, and later during the long vac from Cambridge..."

"I shan't be here after next week, Robert. I'm going to London."

She saw that the news came as a stunning blow to Robert, leaving him momentarily speechless. When he had recovered somewhat, he seized both her hands, crying out, "I won't let you go, I can't let you go..."

Leonie gently disengaged herself. "I must go. There's no place for me here now."

"But I don't understand, mademoiselle,—Leonie—I love you. I was going to wait to tell you until I was a little older, but... Leonie, my dearest, I want you to marry me. Then there'll be no need for you to leave Wanstead Abbey."

Aghast, Leonie thought quickly, knowing that she must choose her words carefully if she were to avoid a mortal injury to Robert's young self-esteem. She rose, gaining a few moments respite by pacing back and forth before the fireplace, before turning back to Robert. "I'm touched and honoured by your offer," she said at last, "and I thank you for it. But while you're underage, there is no way that you can be married legally without your stepmother's consent. And you know that she would never consent to your marriage to me."

"Yes, I know that," said Robert eagerly, "but we could elope. No, wait, please—hear me out. An elopement to Gretna Green isn't at all the thing—I realise that a certain amount of scandal always attaches to such ceremonies—but consider: I'm told that, once a couple is actually married over the border, the families are usually forced to accept the situation. After all, any attempt to undo the marriage would only result in even greater scandal."

Suppressing a sigh, Leonie said quietly, "Even so, there would be a great deal of unpleasantness. Lady Linton would move heaven and earth to nullify such a marriage. Then there is the matter of money. Your stepmother controls your fortune until you reach your majority. What would we live on until you became twenty-one?"

"My grandmother left me a small income. We could scrape by on that. And Mama would eventually have to come around," said Robert doggedly. "Once she was convinced that we truly loved each other..."

"Ah, Robert, there's the real reason we can't get married. I would do anything not to hurt you, but there is only one way to say this: I don't love you. I'm fond of you—*very* fond of you—but that is all."

"But it's a beginning. I know that I can make you love me, if you'll just let me try."

"No, Robert. You'll cause me great pain if you won't accept my answer as final."

It seemed to Leonie that Robert slipped into adulthood before her very eyes. He turned quite pale, but he squared his shoulders and with a touching young dignity said, "You're quite right. It was unpardonable of me to press you like this. Please forgive me. You'll still allow me to be your friend?"

"Oh, Robert, of course I will."

"Thank you. And will you write to me occasionally?"

Steeling her heart, Leonie shook her head. "You know how much Lady Linton would disapprove of any correspondence between us. If she found out about it she might make it very difficult for me to hold another position."

"I hadn't thought about that. I presume Mama is quite capable of such spite," replied Robert out of his fledgling maturity. "But you will let me see you at least once more, won't you? To say good-bye? And perhaps there might be something I could do to help with your moving preparations?"

"No. I thank you for your kind thoughts, but I can manage very well," Leonie exclaimed, anxious to avoid any further provocation of the viscountess. But then, observing Robert's crestfallen expression, she added impulsively, "There *is* one great favour you could do me: would you drive me to Winchester to catch the stagecoach for London?"

Robert beamed, his dejection slipping away. "I'll be happy to do that—more than happy, delighted."

"Thank you. Shall we say Monday next, then? Very early, about five in the morning?"

As Robert turned to leave, he spotted the miniatures that Leonie had placed on the kitchen table on his arrival. "Are these your parents? Yes, they must be—the lady looks so much like you." He picked up the miniatures, studying them carefully. "They changed a great deal as they grew older, didn't they? I should hardly have recognised either of them."

"Yes, they did change. It was the grief, and the illness, I suppose." As she spoke, Leonie realised that by allowing Robert to believe that the portraits in the miniatures were those of Armand de Montbarey and his wife, she had already made the decision not to reveal to anyone the truth of her parentage—or lack of it. She set her jaw firmly. She would leave the village with her head set proudly, ready to carve a new future for herself with the same courage that Armand had shown when he followed the banners of Condé to defeat at Valmy.

2

"I MEANT TO tell you earlier, you're looking very lovely this morning," observed Robert, gazing at Leonie across the table in the crowded coffee room of the Anchor Inn in Winchester.

Leonie coloured, glancing down at her pelisse of grey kerseymere, worn over a simple dress of lavender-coloured jaconet muslin. Compliments were new to her, for there had been an almost total lack of emphasis on personal appearance in her father's austere household. But, as she had peered into her mirror that morning to adjust her beehive straw bonnet, she had experienced a slightly guilty pleasure in the thought that she *was* looking quite pretty in the new clothes she had bought to replace her shabby black mourning dresses.

"I'm glad to see that you've left off your blacks," Robert went on.

"Yes, I must put my best foot forward now. I'm afraid that a funereal appearance would discourage a prospective employer..." She broke off. Robert's eyes were fixed on an object behind her left shoulder, and his expression was decidedly hostile.

"Is there something wrong, Robert?"

Returning his attention to her, Robert growled, "I don't like the way that fellow's been staring at you, mademoiselle. Lombard Street to a China orange, he's one of those Bond Street Loungers. I've a notion to land him a facer."

Leonie turned her head slightly. There, at the table next to theirs, sat a young man dressed in extremely bright yellow pantaloons, with shirt points so high that he could scarcely turn his head and, instead of a neck cloth, a spotted Belcher handkerchief knotted carelessly about his neck. She had observed his entry earlier into the coffee room and had marvelled at his dandified appearance, so strange to her country eyes.

"Please don't do anything rash, Robert. Even if he *is* staring at me, I'll just keep my back turned to him and that will be the end of it."

Robert reluctantly looked away from the young dandy. "Very well, I won't do anything to embarrass you, but I still don't like it by half. The thing is you shouldn't be travelling alone like this, without a maid, or a companion..." He cocked his head as the repeated blasts of a horn sounded in the distance. "The Exeter stage is right on time," he said consulting his pocket watch. "Let's be off."

Outside in the courtyard there was a bustle of disciplined activity as the stagecoach, its horn blasts growing ever louder and more peremptory, swept through the gates of the inn. Immediately hostlers swarmed in to unhitch the four-horse teams as other hostlers brought up its replacement. The guard laid down his horn and scrambled from his high perch on the boot to help a departing passenger retrieve his luggage and to place Leonie's corded trunk and portmanteau in the wooden baggage compartment at the rear of the coach.

"They'll be off in five minutes—they're very efficient," said Robert, misery lengthening his young face. "Good-bye, mademoiselle. Have a safe journey and—please don't forget me."

"Of course I shan't. Dear Robert, thank you for your many kindnesses and especially for driving me into Winchester this morning. And say good-bye to your sisters for me. Give them my love—and save some for yourself.

Moments later, after Leonie had taken her place in the coach, and the only other passenger to board at Winchester— the young dandy of the coffee room—had climbed up to take his place beside the driver, the stagecoach moved out from the courtyard. Peering back at Robert's forlorn figure, Leonie's eyes misted and there was a sudden hollow feeling in her stomach as she realised that she was cutting the last familiar tie to the place where she had spent most of her life.

Soon, however, her spirits lifted with the pleasurable novelty of travelling, and she began to look about her with interest as they moved past the medieval cathedral in its peaceful close and the nearby Great Hall—the remains of Winchester Castle, where, in one room, Leonie had heard, could still be seen the round oaken table of King Arthur and his knights.

The other occupants of the coach—three elderly gentlemen— sat with their eyes closed, catching up on their rest. Leonie, however, was too keyed up, too exhilarated, to relax. She sat wide-eyed, enjoying the lovely undulating Hampshire countryside as the coach journeyed past tiny villages with thatched whitewashed cottages, overgrown with honeysuckle and roses, clustered around the church and the village green; past prosperous farms and herds of grazing sheep and cattle, through bustling market towns crowded with field workers in straw hats and round smocks and country women in their scarlet cloaks and black silk bonnets behind market tables laden with produce.

In midafternoon, as they stopped for a change of horses, Leonie stepped into the inn yard to stretch her legs. The bright May sun had disappeared behind lowering clouds and she pulled her pelisse closer around her against the steadily decreasing temperature. One of the middle-aged passengers paused beside her and observed, glancing up at the sky, that they would have a storm before long. Then, staring at the young dandy in the spotted Belcher handkerchief, who was just climbing back to his seat beside the driver, the passenger said resentfully, "Well, if that isn't the outside of enough. The driver is allowing that young Pink of the Fancy to ride beside him on the box again."

Leonie looked at him inquiringly. The stagecoach carried only four passengers inside, with one passenger customarily sitting beside the driver and four others on the roof. "I don't understand. The young man has been occupying that place since he boarded the stagecoach in Winchester."

"So he has," replied the man, even more resentfully. "But one of the outside passengers tells me that the driver has been allowing him to take the reins—and since the young looby has been slurping down Blue Ruin at each coach stop, he's now drunk as a wheelbarrow. If he takes the reins again he'll have us all in the ditch, and so I just informed the driver. But there, our rights and comfort count for naught, as you can see."

"But why would the driver allow a passenger to take the reins?" asked Leonie, puzzled.

"Why, for money, of course. It's become all the crack for these nonpareils to drive the stagecoach. They slip some blunt to the drivers, and then, once they are out of town on an open stretch of road, they take over the reins."

"Well, perhaps the driver will take heed to your warning,"

said Leonie soothingly. "There's no place else for the young man to sit, after all."

Once in motion, the stagecoach passed into Surrey, with its heathery commons and forests of beech trees. After they left Farnham, their speed picked up significantly, and soon, as they barrelled down the heavily rutted road, the coach began swaying wildly from side to side. Clutching his hat as he attempted to keep his balance, Leonie's acquaintance exclaimed angrily, "There, I told you so. That young hedge bird is cutting up a lark again. I give him five minutes before he runs us off the road."

It was rather less than five minutes before the passenger was proved right. Suddenly the coach gave a violent lurch and collapsed, not into the ditch, but sideways on the road. Leonie was thrown heavily on top of one of the other passengers, and outside she could hear wails from the poor wretches who had been riding on the roof. With considerable difficulty the occupants of the coach managed to push open the door and clamber up and out, with the driver and the guard assisting them to climb down between the upended wheels.

"Well, now, accidents will happen, but nobody's seriously hurt, so all's well that ends well," said the obviously chastened driver. "We'll have that there wheel fixed and be back on the road again in a trice or my name ain't Jack Sumner.'

But it was obvious even to Leonie's unpracticed eye that the wheel in question would not be fixed in a trice. It had not merely been wrenched off but was badly splintered. As the chilled passengers huddled forlornly by the side of the road and the driver and guard wrestled ineffectually with the wheel, a strong wind rose, the sky became even darker, and rain began to fall.

Leonie walked up to the driver. "Are we very far from the

next stop? Could I walk there and wait under shelter until you have the wheel fixed?"

"That might be best, ma'am. We'll be a mile, or perhaps two, from Guildford. We change horses at the Angel Inn."

With the rain coming down even more heavily, Leonie started off. Her straw bonnet was already limp and she realised that she would be soaked through before she ever reached Guildford, but anything was preferable to standing around in the mud beside the grounded stagecoach. Within a minute or two she could hear the sound of wheels coming up behind her, and she moved to the side of the road to allow the carriage to pass. The vehicle, a sporting curricle with its hood up, stopped a short distance ahead of her, however, and a very small man dressed in groom's livery hopped down and walked back to her. He touched his hand to his cap, saying, "Master wishes to know if you'd like a ride to Guildford, ma'am."

"No, I thank you," Leonie exclaimed automatically, every instinct rejecting the thought of accepting a ride from a complete stranger. But then as another, stronger gust of wind sent her to shivering, she said hastily, "Yes, I would like that very much."

"Come along then, ma'am." Leonie followed the groom to the curricle, where the little man helped her mount the iron step to the driver's seat and disappeared behind the carriage. Leonie turned to the driver, a youngish man whose strongly handsome features were framed by fashionably disarranged curls of black hair. He wore a drab many-caped driving coat, a high-crowned beaver hat, and breeches with beautifully polished top boots. "I must thank you for playing the Good Samaritan, sir," she said shyly. "When the stagecoach broke down I was resigned to waiting at the roadside until the wheel was fixed, but then, when it began to rain..."

"Not at all. Happy to oblige," murmured the driver with a

measuring glance from his cool grey eyes. His words were perfectly polite, but uttered in tones of such bland indifference that Leonie, acutely aware of her limp bonnet and her damp pelisse, began to feel like the most ignorant of country servant girls alongside this obvious nonpareil.

A thought struck her. "Your groom," she said anxiously. "I'm sure he must have been riding beside you, out of the rain..."

"My tiger is standing on the perch behind the hood, his usual place. He doesn't mind a little rain, I assure you. Or if he does, it's no matter. Jim's paid to do what he's told," replied the driver with the same icy indifference as he flicked the horses into motion, displaying, even to Leonie's unaccustomed eyes, a sure mastery over the two magnificent, beautifully matched animals.

Chilled, both literally and figuratively, Leonie lapsed into silence, sinking back against the seat, happy to have the hood between herself and the rain, which was now pelting down harder than ever. She felt a twinge of pity for her still stranded fellow passengers, and, as she gazed ahead of her at the road, its rutted surface becoming a quagmire of mud, she reflected on how uncomfortable her ride in the stagecoach would have been even if the vehicle had not lost a wheel.

Soon the curricle was turning into the High Street of the little town that Leonie took to be Guildford. "Would you let me off at the Angel, please?" she asked the driver, breaking the long, and what had been to her an uncomfortable, silence. "The coach will be coming here once it's repaired."

"As a matter of fact, I'll be stopping here myself," replied the driver, guiding the curricle through the gates of the Angel Inn into the galleried courtyard. "I don't fancy continuing on to London tonight in this downpour."

As the curricle came to a stop, and despite the driving rain, a pair of hostlers rushed out to take the horses, with several porters in their wake to take charge of the luggage. The tiger, Jim, leaped from his perch to assist Leonie down from the curricle. She scurried from the courtyard into the inn, almost into the arms of the smiling landlord, waiting to welcome his guests at the door. His smile faded somewhat as he gazed at her bedraggled clothing, but rekindled when he caught sight of her companion, striding unhurriedly into the inn, giving his beaver hat a slight shake to shed the raindrops before settling it back on his carefully arranged curls.

"Mr. Deveril! A hearty welcome to you, sir," exclaimed the landlord.

"Evening, Burleigh. Do you have a room for me? Those roads out there are becoming impassable."

"Oh, indeed, sir. The maids will prepare your room immediately. And I'll reserve the private parlour for your dinner, of course." He looked dubiously at Leonie. "The lady, sir—is she with you?"

Leonie intervened hastily. "I'm travelling alone. That is, Mr. Deveril kindly gave me a lift when the stagecoach broke a wheel. Could I have a room, please, just for a few hours until the stagecoach is repaired and I can continue my journey? I would like to dry my clothes."

The landlord's cordiality seemed to dissolve. "You left your maid with the stagecoach, Madame?" he asked, pursing his lips and casting another long, slow look at her simple clothes, now much the worse for the elements.

"No, of course not. I don't have a maid. I told you, I'm travelling alone, sir," said Leonie with a rising sense of annoyance.

Mr. Burleigh shook his head. "I'm very sorry, ma'am. We're full up. I don't have a room to give you."

From the landlord's cursory tone, Leonie realised that she was the victim of a snobbish prejudice against single females of modest means travelling alone by public conveyance—a universal prejudice, she was to learn later, which extended to all stagecoach and wagon passengers, and which often resulted in poor service and downright bad food and bed. Landlords much preferred the prestige and higher profits of catering to the "swells" travelling by private carriage.

"Couldn't you possibly give me a room for a short while, an hour or two? The merest cupboard would do," Leonie began, knowing full well that she was not likely to change the landlord's mind. But even as Mr. Burleigh started to shake his head again, his mind was changed for him by Mr. Deveril's incisive voice, saying, "Come now, Burleigh, that's doing it rather too brown—you must have a room somewhere saved for that very special guest. Please oblige me by giving it to the lady."

"Certainly, Mr. Deveril. I'll be happy to find something for Miss—uh, Miss..."

"My name is Leonie de Montbarey."

"Yes, indeed, Miss de Montbarey. I didn't know, Mr. Deveril, do y'see, that Miss de Montbarey was a friend of yours..." His voice trailed off as Mr. Deveril, ignoring the landlord's anxious apologies, tipped his hat to Leonie with a slight bow and murmured, "At your service, ma'am," and went off up the stairs after the maid.

Leonie watched him go with mixed feelings. On the one hand, she knew that, without his intervention, she would have been left to wait in her damp clothes for hours, or until whenever the stagecoach arrived at the inn; on the other hand, she found herself resenting his easy arrogance, his unquestioning assumption that he need only lift his voice to have his wishes gratified.

An hour later, however, she had put her resentment behind her, feeling much more the thing as the little chambermaid brought back her dress, dried and neatly ironed. Remembering Robert's seasonal advice, to be generous in her vails to the inn servants, she tipped the maid lavishly and was rewarded by a beaming smile. She donned the dress and eased her feet into the light slippers that had been toasting beside the fireplace, relieved that most of the dampness had evaporated. Combing her hair into its usual smooth curls, and leaving her pelisse to continue drying by the fire, Leonie, suddenly remembering that she had had only a cup of tea and a biscuit since an early breakfast, went down the stairs in search of the coffee room.

She stood at the entrance of the coffee room, somewhat nervous at the sound of raucous laughter from a group of young men occupying a table in the corner. Peering about for a vacant place at one of the other tables, she realised with a sinking feeling that she was the only woman present.

"There you are, my dear. I was wondering where you'd got to."

Leonie turned her head in affronted surprise to find herself accosted by the young man in the spotted Belcher handkerchief whose inexpert driving had caused the stagecoach to lose a wheel. His once dandyish clothes were in a sad state from the rain and the mud, and he appeared even more intoxicated than he had earlier in the day.

"Good evening, sir," said Leonie coldly. "Has the stagecoach been repaired?"

"Lord, no," grinned the young man. "The wheel is so badly splintered that it will have to be replaced. It will take hours—perhaps all night—before we start off again. So we—the rest of the passengers—decided to follow your example and take shelter at the Angel. We didn't have your good fortune—no rides in sporting curricles for us! But here we are, finally. Come have some supper with us." As he spoke, the young man placed his hand on Leonie's arm.

Leonie pulled away. "Thank you, no," she said, even more coldly. "I prefer to eat by myself."

"You can't mean that. Why dine alone when you can be with friends?"

"You are not my friend," snapped Leonie. "What's more, you're intoxicated."

"I am not foxed," protested the young man in injured tones. "A trifle concerned, perhaps, but not castaway. *I* know," he added, inspired, "you just want to be coaxed, ma'am. That's it, isn't it? So consider yourself coaxed and come join us." He tugged again at her arm, and Leonie, outraged, and unable to pull her arm from his determined grip, lashed out at him with a sharp kick to the shins which caused him to lose his unsteady balance. As he lurched away from her, Mr. Deveril appeared behind him, laying a firm hand on the young man's shoulder. "The lady doesn't seem to care for your company," said Mr. Deveril. "I should advise you to look elsewhere for companionship."

A ripple of laughter ran through the coffee room. The young man, turning a bright red, said hotly, "I'll thank you not to interfere in my affairs, sir." Then, as Deveril failed to reply, merely raising an amused eyebrow, the dandy lunged toward him, swinging his right fist. Deveril, moving his head and shoulder ever so slightly to avoid the blow, reached out, smoothly and effortlessly, to land a right-handed blow to the dandy's head.

"Very pretty, Mr. Deveril," commented the landlord, gazing down at the young man, who lay on the floor, blinking his unfocused eyes. "You've drawn his cork proper. A pity that you didn't darken both his daylights while you were about it."

"Oh, I never expend more than the necessary effort," replied Deveril. He turned to Leonie. "You may rest easy now, ma'am," he said. "I fancy your admirer will cause you no more trouble."

Already unhappily aware that she was the object of every inquisitive and staring eye in the room, Leonie cringed at the note of easy condescension in Deveril's voice. "I thank you for your—your assistance," she said stiffly," even though it was quite unnecessary. I was perfectly capable of dealing with the problem myself."

"Yes, I saw the kick you aimed at our friend's shin," said Deveril with another slightly amused lift of his eyebrow. He glanced about the coffee room. "If I might make a suggestion, ma'am, this place seems far too crowded, especially for a lady eating alone—would you care to dine with me in my private parlour?"

"Thank you. You are too kind. I find, however, that I am not really very hungry, after all. I think I will just go up to my room."

"As you wish, but after your—ah—rather strenuous experiences today, it would be strange indeed if you were not just a trifle hungry." He eyed Leonie with a faint smile. "I assure you that I haven't the faintest of designs on your person. Burleigh here will tell you that I'm a gentleman of unblemished reputation. We will leave the door of the room open, if you like."

Bridling at the tinge of gentle mockery in Deveril's expression, Leonie's first reaction was to stalk angrily past him, but then, as a serving maid walked past her bearing a platter of roast beef, her stomach contracted and she realised that she felt hungry to the point of lightheadedness. And what would be the harm, after all, in dining with Mr. Deveril? She would have some privacy, after the strain of the day, and who was there to point the finger at her for being unladylike, when, after this evening, she would never lay eyes on him again?

"On second thought, I've changed my mind, sir," she said, still stiffly. "I would like to accept your invitation."

A little later, as she sat sipping an excellent Madeira before a roaring fire in the comfortable private parlour, watching the serving maid place an excellent dinner on the table—soup, a

leg of mutton with pastry pudding, a duck, fresh asparagus—
Leonie was glad that she had overcome her scruples about
associating with a stranger. Mr. Deveril was behaving with an
exemplary, almost impersonal courtesy. He helped her to the
mutton, urged her to another serving of asparagus, refilled
her wine glass, all the while making the most unexceptional
of small talk.

'The Angel does one very well,'' he observed. ''I've never
had a poor dinner here. But of course, it's not surprising.
They've been serving travellers for centuries.''

"Then I'm fortunate that I had an accident only a short
distance form here,'' replied Leonie, somewhat shyly. It was
the first time that she had ever eaten a meal alone with a man
other than her father; indeed, it was the first time that she had
ever had any kind of prolonged contact with a man. Except
for Robert, of course, and she had always thought of Robert
more as a large child than as an adult. ''And I was doubly
fortunate that you came along as the Good Samaritan to offer
me a ride here. I fear that the other passengers were soaked to
the skin.''

''No more than some of them deserved, I daresay. The
landlord tells me that the gossip in the coffee room is to the
effect that the young hedge bird I had to mill down was
responsible for the accident to the stagecoach. I cannot
fathom the logic behind their thinking,'' he added in thoughtful distaste, ''but your callow, would-be dandy has only to
crack a bottle or two and he thinks that he can drive to an
inch.''

Over the apricot tart and fresh fruit and cheese Leonie
began to feel more at ease and even to enjoy her unconven-
tional experience.

''I just realised that I've been very remiss, ma'am—I
haven't introduced myself properly,'' said her companion,
rising and giving her a slight bow before resuming his seat.

"My name is Deveril—Jeremy Deveril. And I believe that you told the landlord that your name is Montbarey. Do I detect the slightest of French accents? Or, rather, an intonation? May I hazard the guess that you belong to an émigré family?"

"I do, yes. My father was Baron Armand de Montbarey. He came to England with my mother and me after the army of the Prince de Condé was defeated at Valmy. I was little more than a baby then, of course. I have no recollection of our life in France. My memories begin with our stay in the Winchester area."

"It's rather unusual to find an émigré family so far from London. Most of them tended to congregate near each other in certain areas of London—whole sections of the parish of St. Marylebone, for example, are almost totally French speaking." At Leonie's look of surprise he smiled and added, "I know a little about the émigré situation—my father served on the French Committee during the nineties and worked quite closely with Mr. Wilmot in attempting to alleviate the worst of the problems encountered by the émigrés. Father always said that he considered it little short of insult to offer these proud people only a shilling a day per person for their total support. I understand that many of them had to engage in quite menial occupations to augment that shilling a day."

"So my parents have told me. They always felt fortunate that they were able to find congenial employment, Father as a tutor and fencing instructor, and *Maman* as a teacher of the piano."

"You say 'were.' Are your parents then not living?"

"No. Father died almost a year ago, my mother some years before that."

"I'm very sorry to hear that." He reached over to replenish her wine glass. "Are you travelling to London to visit friends, Mlle. de Montbarey?"

"No, Mr. Deveril. I hope to find employment there."

Mr Deveril lifted an eyebrow. "Employment? In what capacity, may I ask?"

"As a governess."

"Indeed? And do you have experience as a governess?"

"Certainly," said Leonie rather shortly. She was beginning to feel uncomfortable again under Deveril's coolly penetrating gaze, becoming more aware that she had placed herself in an ambiguous position in agreeing to dine with him. She was quite positive that no lady who shared Mr. Deveril's social standing would have been subjected to this offhand interrogation. "I have acted as governess for the past two years to Viscount Linton's daughters," she said, looking at him with a slightly defiant lift to her chin.

"Is that so? I knew Lord Linton slightly. I was sorry to hear of his recent death. He was a fine man."

"Yes, he was. I was very happy at Wanstead Abbey."

"There's that past tense again. Am I to conclude that you ceased to be happy at Wanstead Abbey?"

Leonie flushed. "Lady Linton has decided to make a change," she said stiffly. Then she added, unable to keep a tinge of bitterness out of her voice, "The viscountess prefers someone with different qualifications."

"And what sort of qualifications does she have in mind?"

"Lady Linton would like her daughters to learn netting, and painting on fans, wax work and lace making—important skills like that," Leonie said scathingly.

"Ah." Mr. Deveril cocked his head. "You sound as though you do not prize such accomplishments, Mlle. de Montbarey."

"Not at all," protested Leonie. "It's just that I also place importance on music, languages, history and literature. My father, Mr. Deveril, thought that women should be able to use their minds, too." She stopped, biting her lip. "I beg your pardon. I shouldn't be boring you with my ideas."

"Please don't apologise. You're entitled to any opinion you care to hold." Deveril paused, narrowing his eyes as he gazed at Leonie with another of those long, considering, faintly amused stares. "I seem to recall that Lady Linton has a stepson—sixteen years of age, eighteen years, something like that," he said after a moment. The smile broadened. "Could it possibly be that the viscountess is less concerned about her daughters' education than about her stepson's—er—growth into maturity?"

Turning an angry red, Leonie wondered fleetingly if Mr. Deveril possessed the evil eye, enabling him to read the minds of his victims. She jumped up, exclaiming in a choked voice, "That was an ungentlemanly thing to say, Mr. Deveril. I collect that it wouldn't have crossed your mind to say it to someone you considered your social equal. I'll thank you for your hospitality—which, I assure you, was a very mixed blessing—and bid you good night." She turned on her heel, about to sweep out of the room, when Deveril, standing up, reached out his hand to catch her wrist.

"Mlle. de Montbarey, you're quite right, that was an ungentlemanly thing to say. I beg your pardon. I have an arrogant habit of saying whatever idle thought crosses my mind—I'm worse even than Brummell, so my friends tell me. Will you forgive me? And sit down again to finish your wine?"

Leonie hesitated, but then, as she saw no trace of mockery in his expression, she said in a small voice, "I accept your apology, sir."

"Thank you, that is most generous of you." As Leonie sat down opposite him, Deveril said, 'I truly don't wish to be intrusive, but I would like to make amends for my faux pas by being helpful to you in some way, if I can. Tell me, do you have a promise of employment in London?"

"No. I thought I would answer advertisements in the

newspapers, register at the Labour Exchange, perhaps contact some of my parents' old friends in the French community..."

"I see. Do you have a place to stay? No? Might I suggest, then, a possible lodging—my family's former housekeeper is now married to the proprietor of a pastry shop in Mayfair, off Bond Street. I think that she would be very willing to rent you a room."

"Thank you, you're very kind, but I couldn't possibly accept..."

Leonie's refusal was made almost instinctively. Deveril shrugged, reverting to his former air of cool indifference. "Do as you like, of course. I would have thought it might be helpful to you to have a respectable lodging on your first visit to London, but..." He walked over to the writing desk in the corner of the room and, taking out his card case, wrote briefly on one of his cards. He came back, placing the card on the table in front of her. "There is the address of my former housekeeper, if you should change your mind. Good night, Mlle. de Montbarey. I wish you a pleasant journey to London."

Mr. Deveril left the room, leaving Leonie feeling quite flustered, like a fool or a very young child. She picked up the card, giving it a long, thoughtful look.

3

"Come Along, Miss Leonie, and have have your ham and eggs while they're still warm," urged Mrs. Kirby as Leonie came into her bright kitchen.

"Mrs. Kirby, I wish you would let me make my own breakfast," protested Leonie. "You have more than enough to do without waiting on me hand and foot."

"Nonsense, my dear. Young ladies like yourself don't belong in the kitchen," said Mrs. Kirby, as she bustled over to pour Leonie's tea.

Leonie sighed. It had proved practically impossible to convince Mrs. Kirby that her young lodger was indeed a member of the working class. A few moments in Leonie's company sufficed for Mrs. Kirby to appraise her prospective paying guest's graceful, well-bred manners and soft, precise voice and to conclude that this was a gentlewoman, however straitened her economic circumstances might be. Her attitude toward Leonie was very like that of a priviledge upper servant toward the daughter of the house.

Leonie watched the woman's plump, middle-aged form as she moved energetically about the kitchen, making the day's first batch of the pastries that had made the little shop she operated with her husband so successful. In addition to their many kinds of pastries, they sold forced fruits, orgeat and lemonade, and the shop was a popular lunchtime gathering place for the Bond Street Loungers in their tight pantaloons, high starched shirt points and elaborately tied cravats. It took Leonie only a short time to identify these dandies as the models for poor Robert's attempts at modish dressing on his last visit home from Harrow.

"Will you be going out today, Miss Leonie, or will you be staying here to write letters?" asked Mrs. Kirby in one of her infrequent pauses, as she brushed the perspiration from her forehead with a flour-smudged forearm.

"I've written so many letters that I've quite lost track of them," said Leonie ruefully. "I've answered every single advertisement in the *Morning Post* and the *Times* that seemed the least bit promising. And yet, here I am, six weeks after I arrived in London, and I still don't have a position."

"But you've received a number of answers, that I know, Miss Leonie."

"Oh, yes, but they were all turn-downs. I suspect that my age is my biggest handicap, but most employers seem to want the drawing and fancywork skills, too, which I don't have."

"What about the interview you had yesterday—that call from the Registry Office?"

"The same old story. Mrs. Adams said that I was too young."

Mrs. Kirby shook her head wisely. "There was probably an impressionable younger son in the Adams establishment. Employers don't want young, beautiful governesses about the place if they have unmarried sons. Well I remember that Mrs. Deveril, when she had to replace Miss Caroline's governess, chose an older lady principally because, as she told me herself, Master Jeremy was just at the susceptible age."

Leonie's quick blush faded as she realised that Mrs. Kirby, who could have no inkling of the circumstances that had led to Leonie's dismissal by Lady Linton, was simply indulging in her favorite pastime of reminiscing about her years of service with the Deveril family. Leonie leaned back to listen, reflecting that Mrs. Kirby might well have married in late middle age only partly to have a home of her own; it may have been that she was simply lonely at the Deveril country estate, with both her employers dead, the daughter of the house married and Jeremy, as she had so often told Leonie, off spending his time as a dashing man about town.

"Not but what Mrs. Deveril wasn't quite right about Master Jeremy," Mrs. Kirby chuckled knowingly. "He started in the petticoat line while he was still at Eton. We never really knew why he was sent down from Cambridge, but I'll wager it was the wenching as well as the high jinks and the drinking. It was then that old Mr. Deveril, exasperated, as well he might be, decided to buy Master Jeremy a commission and pack him off to the army. But then, of course, brother Arthur died, and Jeremy became the heir, not only to his father's estate but the Winchcombe title. I told you about the old earl, didn't I, Miss Leonie?"

"Oh, yes, yes you did," replied Leonie hastily. And, indeed, she had heard the story more than once. Jeremy Deveril, who had inherited from his father a small but prosperous estate, as Mrs. Kirby had impressively informed her, was one day going to be among the wealthiest men in England. The family relationships were complex, but Leonie had gathered that Jeremy's grandfather and the present Earl of Winchcombe were first cousins, so that the earl, though Mrs. Kirby commonly referred to him as Jeremy's uncle, was more properly a distant cousin. Jeremy's father and grandfather were both dead, and, since the earl was childless, Jeremy was now the heir to his vast estates.

"Not but what the old earl could still marry and have children," Mrs. Kirby went on, "I collect he's not much more than sixty years old, after all, but no one seems to expect him to marry again—his wife died many years ago— and I must say, for the sake of Jeremy and Miss Caroline, that I hope he doesn't. I really don't know how poor Miss Caroline would have managed, all these years, if the earl hadn't interested himself in her affairs."

Mrs. Kirby rambled on about Caroline and her family, giving some new details, repeating others, until Leonie began to feel almost as familiar with the Deverils as if she had met them in the flesh. It seemed that Caroline, a lovely girl, but quite different in her quiet, dreamy way from her strong-willed younger brother, had married very advantageously, or so everyone had thought, the Marquis of Ashbury. At first it had seemed a very happy marriage, with Caroline giving birth to a numerous family. But alas, Lord Ashbury had turned out to be both a libertine and a gambler; after his death some years previously, it was learned that the family fortune was gone and the Ashbury estate heavily in debt.

"Of course, Miss Caroline's been able to depend for help and advice on Mr. Jeremy," said Mrs. Kirby. "He's worked with the agent so that the Ashbury estates are being managed properly again, and he's very interested in the children. But it's the old earl, so I hear, who's made the difference for Miss Caroline. He settled Lord Ashbury's most pressing debts, and he's paying for the heir's—young John's—studies at Cambridge, and for Miss Fanny's dowry when she married last year. And the last time I saw Miss Caroline—she comes to see me whenever she's in London—she hinted that the earl was prepared to buy Thomas's commission in a line regiment."

"Lady Ashbury is very fortunate to have such a generous relative," Leonie murmured.

"Isn't she, just! But there, Miss Leonie, I've been running on quite long enough. Have you decided on your plans for today?"

"Could I give you a hand in the shop? I noticed yesterday that you were very rushed at the luncheon hour."

"Lord, no, I couldn't allow you to do a thing like that," said Mrs. Kirby, shocked. "What would Mr. Jeremy think if I allowed you to serve customers in the shop?"

Leonie gave a helpless shrug. Quite simply, Mrs. Kirby could not grasp the fact that it was necessary for her lodger to earn her own living. "Then, if you don't need my help," Leonie said, "I think I will pay a visit to one of my parents' old friends, the Comtesse de Vaucouleurs. If the comtesse is still living in London, she might be able to advise me about finding a position."

As Leonie left the pastry shop and turned north on Bond Street, she was soon lost in her usual delight in the infinite variety of the London scene. Since her arrival in the city she had spent many hours strolling through the streets; she watched the dandies driving their elegant carriages or sauntering to their clubs in St. James' Street, paused before the opulent mansions in Mayfair and Grosvenor Square and lingered in front of the fashionable shops in Pall Mall and Piccadilly. She marvelled at the new gas lighting, newly installed that very year of 1809, and became accustomed to the incessant clatter of hooves and iron wheels on the well-paved streets. Most of all she gazed in fascinated interest at the sheer exuberant life of the noisy, congested streets, with their ballad singers and street pedlars and beggars, their rabble of crippled soldiers and sailors, prostitutes and chimney sweeps. She still shuddered at the memory of the man who, for a fee, would swallow one of the vipers he kept in a bag, and she gazed with pity at the derelicts who reeled about the streets after their bouts with cheap gin. She had felt constrained to be careful with her small capital, but she had treated herself to a visit to Madam Tussaud's Wax Museum at the Lyceum in the Strand, where she saw the grisly models fashioned right at the foot of the guillotine in Paris; and she had once taken the cheapest seat at the Royal Italian Opera House in the Haymarket to hear an opera by Gluck because she could remember her parents' tales of scrimping on the very food they put in their mouths to hear again one of the operas made so popular by their beloved Marie Antoinette.

Proceeding north on Bond Street, Leonie came, after a long walk, to the Oxford Road and the area beyond that—the parish of St. Marylebone—which was new to her. In the High Street she paused, listening almost with disbelief, to the sound of French voices. She was surrounded by throngs of modestly, even shabbily, dressed shoppers, evidently servants out to do the marketing. From one of them she asked for directions to Baker Street, and was soon in a district of modest, narrow three-storied buildings in the classical style. An inquiry at one of the houses brought further directions to the house of the Comtesse de Vaucouleurs—much to Leonie's relief, for the comtesse's last letter to her parents had been written many years before, and it was more than likely that she no longer lived there. Mounting the steps, she rang the bell. An aged maidservant answered her ring, and Leonie sent in the note that she had written beforehand, giving her name and that of her parents. The servant returned immediately, showing Leonie into a simply furnished parlor, one of an apparent pair of rooms on that floor. Leonie waited somewhat nervously until the arrival of a middle-aged woman with a worn, finely boned face, dressed in a plain muslin gown with a frilled "Biggin' cap of white cambric. At Leonie's curtsey, the woman advanced with open arms, kissing her on both cheeks.

"*Ma Chère* Leonie," said the comtesse, holding her at arm's length as she scrutinised Leonie with tired, kindly eyes. "How wonderful to see you again. It has been so many, many years. You were only a baby—two, perhaps three years old—when I last saw you. But come, sit down with me. Tell me all about your parents. Are they well?"

The comtesse shook her head sadly when told of the deaths of Armand de Montbarey and his wife. "So many are gone now," she said. "and sometimes, you know, one is hard put to regret their passing. Their lives, very often, have been so difficult..." Her voice trailed away, and she sat, lost in her thoughts, for a few moments. "But there," she resumed, flashing a smile, "I was falling into the trap that all we French here in London try strenuously to avoid, of feeling sorry for myself. We've had to keep our spirits up, because our lives here are so very different from our old lives in France. Most of us, who literally never had to lift a finger in the old days, have had to turn our hands to earning a living in any way that we can. My friends have opened shops and restaurants, taught fencing and French, made hats and dresses—the Comte de Caumont actually became a bookbinder! I paint water colours, and if I say so myself, they don't sell at all badly!"

Leonie nodded. "I know. Papa became a tutor and *Maman* gave lessons on the pianoforte, and they told me that there were times when they both felt that they were living in some kind of unpleasant dream and would soon wake up to find themselves back in Champagne."

"I just realised that you have something of your mother, especially around the mouth," said the comtesse suddenly, "and that is so strange, really, because..." She broke off, her hand flying to her mouth.

"Please don't feel embarrassed, madame," said Leonie quickly. "I know all about my parentage. Or, rather, I know Papa and *Maman* were not my natural parents."

"Thank you for telling me that, *ma chère*," said the comtesse in relieved tones. "Your poor mother was always so anxious that you would never learn the truth, which I thought a mistake, quite frankly. Have you ever learned anything more about your real mother?"

"Nothing at all. I have her portrait, and what I assume to be my father's portrait, but..." Leonie shrugged. "I don't even know her Christian name."

"Yes, I recall now that your mother showed me those portraits. You come of fine stock, Leonie, you can be sure of that. And perhaps, one day, when that upstart Bonaparte is removed from the soil of France, you can go back there and search for some clue to your real identity—yes, Marthe, what is it?" The comtesse looked at the card which the old maidservant had just brought in. She turned back to Leonie saying, "The Comte de Morville. I thought you might like to meet him. He knew your parents, too, when he was a young man fresh from serving with the Prince's army."

The handsome, trim-figured, elegantly dressed man who entered the room several moments later appeared to be in his very late thirties or early forties. "But of course I remember the Baron and Baronne de Montbarey," he smiled when the comtesse introduced him to Leonie. "I am grieved to hear of their deaths. And what are you doing in London, mademoiselle, if I may ask?"

"We were just getting to that, monsieur," said the comtesse, motioning her guests to chairs as Marthe brought in a tray with hot chocolate and little cakes. "Are you just here for a visit, Leonie?"

When Leonie described her fruitless efforts to find a position as governess, the comtesse said wisely, "It's as I've always said, dear Leonie—the English really do not care for educated women." She added wistfully, "When I think of the wonderful conversation that we had in those brilliant Parisian salons before 1789..."

"But you, madame, with your 'evenings,' are doing much to preserve those memories," exclaimed the comte gallantly.

"You are much too kind," replied the comtesse, but she was clearly gratified. Returning to Leonie's problems, she said, "I don't know of anything right at this moment, my dear child, but if I should hear of a possible opening for you, I will be sure to inform you. You must tell me where you are staying—Kirby's pastry shop on Brook Street off Bond Street? I shall never remember that, *chérie*. Please go over to the desk and write down your direction for me."

"I believe I know the shop—it has an excellent reputation," said the comte. "In the summer the Kirby's ices rival those of our own Comtesse de Guery!"

When Leonie returned to Brook Street that morning she still felt the glow of the warm welcome she had received from the Comtesse de Vaucouleurs and was not even especially disheartened to read still another letter rejecting her application for a position. She observed that Mrs. Kirby was being swamped in the luncheon rush and insisted on helping to wait on the customers, brushing aside her landlady's familiar plaint of, "Whatever would Mr. Jeremy say?" The thought crossed her mind, in fact, that if worse came to worst and she did not succeed soon in obtaining a post as governess, she might prevail upon Mrs. Kirby to allow her to work for her keep at the shop.

Later that afternoon she was in her room, writing yet another letter of application, when Mrs. Kirby came rushing in to say that a gentleman was there to see her.

"A gentleman? But who could it be?" asked Leonie, puzzled. "Did he come to see me about a position?"

"I'm sure I don't know, Miss Leonie. But do hurry in to the parlour. He's a proper grand gentleman and I'm sure he won't like to be kept waiting."

When Leonie, after hastily brushing her hair and straightening her gown, entered the parlour a few moments later, she was overwhelmed with surprise to see the Comte de Morville, looking exotically out of place in that stiff, painfully neat room.

"I hope you'll forgive me, mademoiselle, for calling on you without an invitation," said the comte with a graceful bow. "I thought, however, that you would wish to know about a possible position that I have in mind for you."

"A position? I fear I don't understand. Surely you can't have learned of a position for me just in the few short hours since I saw you at the home of Mme. de Vaucouleurs."

"You are very perceptive," smiled the comte. "I may sit down? *Merci*. Of course, I did not just learn of this position. I did not broach the subject, however, in the presence of the comtesse, for reasons that I am sure you will readily understand after I explain the situation to you. You see, the position to which I referred is in my own household. I require a governess for my niece, or, rather, for my cousin's child. She calls me 'Uncle' so it is more natural for me to think of Denise as my niece."

"But then, monsieur, I understand you even less than before," protested Leonie, her forehead furrowed into a frown.

"Bear with me, if you please," begged the comte. "Let me tell you Denise's story. Her mother, my cousin, Mme. de Tonneville, was left a widow after the battle of Valmy. She and her child managed to reach the Low Countries along with the other refugees, but once there she was absolutely without funds. She wandered down to the waterfront and saw that an open boat was just leaving for England: she persuaded one of the passengers to take her little daughter, thinking that her child at least might have a chance for safety even if she herself did not. Shortly thereafter she got word to me about her plight, and I of course sent her passage money immediately. But alas, we were not able to locate the child Denise. Mme. de Tonneville became an invalid from the privations of her flight and lived only a few months. However, I never quite abandoned my attempts to find Denise, and, not long ago, I finally did. She had been cared for by a bourgeois family whose small mill had been appropriated by the revolutionaries. They were fine, hard-working people, but almost totally uneducated. As they were, so was Denise: near illiterate, ignorant of all the social niceties. I intend to give Denise every advantage, the home that her lineage entitles her to; but you will understand, I'm sure, why I have not so much as mentioned her name to Mme. de Vaucouleurs. In her present stage Denise resembles nothing so much as a badly trained chambermaid; if I were to present her to my friends before she had acquired at least some of the graces befitting her station, she would be the laughingstock of society. Nothing she might do thereafter to improve herself would bring about her complete acceptance. And yet she is such a lovely girl—she comes from such a distinguished family—do you not think, mademoiselle, that Denise should be helped to realise her full potential? Won't you come to us as her governess?"

The comte's dark eyes focussed on her entreatingly, and his deep voice was warmly persuasive. However, the simple recital of Denise de Tonneville's sad life story would have enlisted Leonie's sympathy in any event. Her heart responded immediately to the girl's plight, in so many ways similar to her own experience.

"I would be happy—no, honoured—to teach Denise," Leonie said, smiling. "In fact, in some strange way, I feel as though I owed her my help. If my adoptive parents hadn't responded so wholeheartedly when my mother died, I might now be even worse off than Denise. Perhaps, in helping her, I may be able to repay just a little of the debt I owe my parents."

"I thank you, mademoiselle," exclaimed the comte. "I was convinced, almost from the first moment I met you, that you were the kind, tenderhearted person I required for my little Denise. When can you come to us? Would tomorrow be too soon?"

"Why, I don't know," began Leonie, taken aback at the comte's enthusiasm. "But why not? There is nothing, after all, to keep me here."

"*Merveilleux!*" approved the comte. "I will send my carriage for you at two o'clock tomorrow afternoon." He took up his hat and stick, preparing to leave. "Oh, there is one thing," he said, pausing at the door. "I should have mentioned it before, I suppose, but—the fact is, you will probably find that teaching Denise will not be easy."

"But how is that?" Leonie looked at the comte with a puzzled frown. "You did say that she was a lovely girl—oh, I think I understand you. Do you mean that Denise is not—not quite bright, is that it?"

"Oh, no, nothing like that, I assure you," replied the comte hastily. "No, Denise has perfectly normal intelligence, as far as I know. The problem is—how shall I put it—that Denise does not really want to learn. You see, she led such a deprived life before I found her, and I, hoping, I suppose, to make it up to her in some way, showered pretty clothes and trinkets upon her, took her to places like Astley's Amphitheatre and Vauxhall Gardens. In short, Denise has grown accustomed to spending her days in primping, shopping, eating the delicacies she never had before, in short, simply enjoying herself. She will, I fear, be most reluctant to change her routine. But I rely on you, mademoiselle; I am sure you are equal to the challenge."

4

PEERING INTO THE swinging glass on the dressing table, Leonie adjusted the frilled white muslin cap that she had taken to wearing indoors, on the theory that it made her look older. Before leaving the bedchamber, she glanced around to make sure that all was in order, feeling the usual rush of pleasure in the elegance and comfort of the room to which she had been assigned in the Comte de Morville's large house in Mount Street, not far, actually, from Mrs. Kirby's pastry shop, but worlds away in fashion. The room contained a four-poster bed, a small washstand, a dressing table, a large wardrobe, several chairs, a dainty writing desk and a large swinging mirror, all constructed in graceful satinwood. Leonie had been relieved at the first sight of her bedchamber, because the rooms on the first floor of the comte's house had been redecorated in the new "classic" style and were rather overwhelming to the untutored eye, with their bright, bold colours—mostly blacks and terra cottas—and furniture decorated with scarabs and lotus flowers and supported on the legs of sphinxes. A sofa in the drawing room had been fashioned in the shape of a crocodile, which Leonie, freely conceding her ignorance in the art of furnishing houses, had privately judged to be going too far.

As she walked down the stairs, Leonie reflected on her initial surprise at the sheer luxury of the comte's house, the upkeep of which obviously required a very large income, since she knew in what straitened circumstances so many of the émigrés in London lived. The mystery had been explained by the comte's "niece," Denise, who told Leonie that the comte had married a wealthy heiress shortly after his arrival in England, and had inherited her fortune when she died several years after the marriage.

Leonie entered the library on the first floor and crossed to the corner to ring the bell. When the footman appeared, she said pleasantly, "Please tell Mademoiselle Denise that it is time for her lesson."

"Certainly, mademoiselle." As the footman closed the door behind him, Leonie shook her head, wondering again why, despite her best efforts, the household staff was not responding to her friendliness. They were never actually impolite, they always performed any task she asked of them, but they remained stiff and unbending, almost as though they resented the addition of another member to the household.

Leonie had a considerable wait before Denise dragged herself into the library, and the young governess suppressed a sigh of exasperation at the sight of her charge's unenthusiastic face. Denise de Tonneville was a striking girl, not tall but with a trim, perfectly proportioned figure, flashing dark eyes and masses of coal-black hair, brought together at the crown of her head and falling in ringlets around her pert face. As usual, however, the pretty face was marred by a mutinous sulk. Decidedly, Denise did not share her uncle's enthusiasm for her education. As the comte had warned Leonie, Denise was almost totally uneducated. She could spell out a few words and she could, with great difficulty, sign her name. Her French was unpolished, her English fluent but ungrammatical, laced with slang and other, ruder sounding expressions that Leonie did not understand and made no effort to decipher.

Leonie had made a valiant effort to teach Denise, giving her lessons from the simple French primers that Leonie's own mother had used, trying to provide at least a smattering of literature and history and some instruction on the piano, but with very little success. Denise simply didn't like books, as she informed Leonie coolly. She would much prefer to go shopping, or to drive through Hyde Park in the comte's carriage.

"*Bonjour*, Denise," Leonie said now. "Did you finish the little story I asked you to read yesterday?"

"No, I didn't, mademoiselle. There were too many big words, and I'm just not interested in elephants, or lions. Why, I don't even like dogs."

Leonie said, trying to keep her voice pleasant, "I'm sorry you weren't interested in the story, Denise. M. de La Fontaine is considered one of the greatest of our French authors."

"But that's just it. Why should I study French authors? I live in England now, and I don't suppose I shall ever live anywhere else."

Leonie gritted her teeth. "The problem, Denise, seems to be that you don't care for English authors either."

Denise seemed quite unconcerned. She sat back in her chair, one hand playing idly with her curls as she replied indifferently, "No, I don't. Why should you be so surprised? I told you when you first came here that I don't like to read. May we go for a little drive this afternoon?"

"Perhaps. Let's see how well the studying goes today." And indeed, for once, the daily session went smoothly; largely because, Leonie thought wryly to herself, they were discussing the reign of Henri IV, and Denise seemed very interested, not in the political events of the period, but in the numerous amatory escapades of the great royal lover.

"Thank you, Denise," said Leonie a little later. "That was a good lesson. Now, let's spend a little time with your music, and then we might consider a drive."

Early on in her task of instructing Denise in singing and the pianoforte, it had become apparent to Leonie that her charge was even less inclined to music than to the rest of her studies; she had a frightfully flat voice, little sense of pitch, and virtually had to be driven to doing any practising at all on the pianoforte.

"Today, as Leonie sat at the instrument, patiently coaching Denise in a simple French folk song, the girl seemed to be in worse voice than usual. The Comte de Morville, who had formed the habit of stopping by almost daily during the schoolroom sessions to check on his ward's progress, slipped into the drawing room as Denise was finishing her song and sat listening to her with a pained expression.

"Enough is enough, mademoiselle," he declared. "Waste no more of your time trying to teach Denise to sing. The voice just isn't there. Concentrate, if you will, on instructing her in the pianoforte. It's a shame, really, because she could have learned so much from you—I can hear that you have a lovely singing voice. Won't you give us the pleasure of hearing you?"

Leonie coloured, glancing at Denise, whose lips were compressed with displeasure. The girl was clearly very attached to her uncle, and, before Leonie's arrival, had apparently received from him nothing but uncritical attention and outright coddling. It had been obvious to Leonie that Denise, on some obscure level and perhaps without at all realising it, resented the transfer of any of the comte's attention from herself to another person.

"Oh, I don't think this is the time or the place for me to sing," Leonie demurred. "We're concerned only with Denise's musical education."

"Precisely my point. You will sing and play for us to demonstrate to Denise how very important musical accomplishment is to a young lady's education."

The comte's smooth, handsome face wore an agreeable smile, but there was a note of cool authority in his voice. Reluctantly, aware of Denise's deepening scowl, Leonie sat down again at the pianoforte. Somewhat nervously she sang, in her clear, high soprano, a captivating little aria by Mozart, *"Welche Wonne, welche Lust,"* which was received enthusiastically by the comte.

"Merveilleux," mademoiselle. Never have I heard that song sung more beautifully. Have you ever attended a performance of *Abduction from the Seraglio?* No? A pity." He paused, knitting his brow. "I have an idea. I can't think why it didn't occcur to me before this. Denise must attend the performance of an opera. We can scarcely wonder at her lack of interest in serious music, when she has never been exposed to it. Wouldn't you agree?"

"I think Denise might profit from hearing an opera, certainly," Leonie replied, rather dubiously. "But I thought it was your policy not to bring her into society until she had acquired more polish."

"Quite right," he nodded. "But in this instance Denise will simply be occupying a place in my box at the Royal Italian Opera House. I will not be introducing her to my friends. No, I've quite made up my mind. The three of us will attend the performance of *Don Giovanni* this evening. You're very fortunate, *ma petite,"* the Comte added smilingly to Denise. "Catalini will be singing the part of Donna Anna. It will be an experience for you to treasure for a lifetime."

There was no great rush of pleasurable expectation to

Denise's face, Leonie noted, but for the moment she disregarded her charge as she said nervously, "Monsieur, I feel that it's quite unnecessary for me to accompany you and Denise to the opera. Unnecessary—and please forgive me for speaking frankly—unsuitable."

The comte lifted an eyebrow. "Unsuitable?" he asked coldly.

Leonie held her ground. "Unusual, at least. Governesses normally don't participate in social occasions with their employers."

"Ah, I see your point," replied the comte, relaxing his hauteur. "But you have obviously not seen mine. This will *not* be a social occasion, as I have already explained. So let me hear no more of these objections."

"I'm sorry, monsieur, but there is one further objection—a very valid one, I'm sure you will agree. I have no dress suitable to wear to the opera."

Briefly considering Leonie's remark, the comte waved his hands dismissingly. "You can wear one of Denise's dresses. You and she are much of a size, and *le Bon Dieu* knows that she has enough of them."

Despite her misgivings, as evening drew near, Leonie discovered that she was actually looking forward to hearing an opera from the vantage of a private box. Denise, too, was becoming excited, not—as she cheerfully informed Leonie—at the prospect of a musical evening but because she relished the thought of "dressing up to the nines."

Even as she gently chided Denise for her use of English slang, Leonie was privately deploring the fact that the girl had so obviously chosen her wardrobe without supervision. Denise's clothes were too ornate, too low-cut, too old for her. The dress she elected to wear to the opera epitomised everything that was wrong with her taste: it was a draped tunic dress of bright red lutestring, embroidered in gold, worn with a toque headdress of red satin crowned with several white crêpe roses and a pair of enormous ostrich plumes. Nothing more unsuitable could be imagined for a young girl who had not yet made her bow in society.

Much to Leonie's relief, she discovered one wearable dress in Denise's wardrobe. Had it been selected, perhaps, by the comte himself, or had Denise been persuaded into purchasing it by a knowledgeable modiste? After she had dressed for the evening, she gazed at herself in the mirror with surprised pleasure: the robe of lavender sarcenet over an embroidered white satin slip, worn with a floating white lace headdress fastened with an aigrette and a white "Chinese" crêpe scarf finished with silk fringe, was the first really fashionable costume she had ever worn and the image in the mirror seemed almost like a stranger to her.

Denise stared at her governess with suddenly narrowed eyes when Leonie knocked at her bedchamber door. "I never liked that dress before," she said thoughtfully. "It seemed so plain. Mousey, really. Madame Vernet practically pressed it on me, or I would never have bought it in the first place. But you look very well in it."

Denise did not sound especially pleased as she spoke; in fact, to Leonie's dismayed ears, there was an undercurrent of jealousy in her voice. Her face brightened, however, as, continuing to gaze at Leonie, she remarked, "I think it must be your colouring—I daresay you couldn't wear a vivid colour like this." She glanced complacently down at herself. "Yes, that must be it, mademoiselle. You must always wear drab colours to avoid looking washed out."

Having thus established in her own mind her superiority over her governess in style and taste, Denise was not particularly put out when, rendezvousing with the two girls in the drawing room, the comte complimented Leonie extravagantly on her appearance. Since the comte also informed Denise that she was looking very striking, the girl was in a festive mood as she and Leonie were handed up the steps into the comte's elegant town carriage. Her high spirits persisted into the performance of the opera, though her appreciation of the occasion obviously owed less to the music itself than to her satisfaction in occupying one of the best boxes at the Royal Italian Opera house. "It costs Uncle 2,500 pounds a season to subscribe to this box," she murmured to Leonie impressively.

After her initial nervousness, when she imagined that everyone in the vast horseshoe-shaped auditorium, with its five tiers of boxes, was staring at her as she entered the comte's box, Leonie lost herself in rapture at the music. The great diva Angelina Catalini, who was singing Donna Anna, was then, at thirty years of age, at the height of her career, a majestic figure with a voice of enormous power. After listening to Catalini sing "*Or Sai chi l'onore,*" Donna Anna's fierce cry for vengeance for her murdered father at the end of Scene 3, Act 1, Leonie sank back against her chair, almost drained of emotion.

At the intermission, the comte leaned over from his chair behind Leonie to ask smilingly, "Are you enjoying the performance, mademoiselle?"

"Oh, monsieur, it's the most thrilling experience of my life," Leonie replied rapturously. "Don't you agree, Denise?"

"I didn't really understand what the story was about," complained Denise. "It would be much better if they sang in English." She raised her opera glasses to her eyes. "Uncle, isn't that the Prince of Wales in the box across from us?"

"It certainly is, *ma petite*," replied the comte, casting a glance of resigned amusement at Leonie as he moved to the box to point out to his niece the main notables who were present in the opera house. But Leonie, her country eyes bedazzled, found herself sharing Denise's excitement in seeing so many of the great and famous on the London scene. There was the heir to the throne, the Prince of Wales, still handsome despite his high colour and many unneeded pounds of flesh; the notorious Lady Lade, once the mistress of "Sixteen String Jack," a highwayman hanged in the 70s; the lovely Lady Jersey, one of the all-powerful patronesses of Almack's Assembly Rooms; the eccentric Henry Cope, whose every article of clothing was a bright green; and even that supreme arbiter of the fashionable scene, the famous Beau Brummell, at first glance so unobtrusive in the plainest of dark-coloured evening wear.

Leonie was startled, when her eye returned to Lady Jersey's box, to see Jeremy Deveril seated in conversation with the countess. He, like Brummell, was dressed in severest black, his handsome head crowned by a fashionably combed "Brutus," and he seemed to be on the friendliest terms with Lady Jersey. More than friendly, thought Leonie, as she watched Deveril lean forward to whisper in his companion's ear, which caused Lady Jersey to veil her face coquettishly with her fan. Leonie watched him closely, until the end of intermission, hoping to catch his eye so that she could exchange a bow and a smile, but his glance never travelled in her direction. Later, after the second act of *Don Giovanni* had begun, she looked back at Lady Jersey's box, but Deveril was no longer there.

"That will be all for today, Denise," said Leonie, several days later, stifling a sigh. She had hoped that Denise's gala evening at the opera might leave the girl more contented, more amenable to instruction, but such had not been the case. Denise was more scatterbrained, less inclined to study, than ever.

As Denise left the library, the comte entered. He wore breeches and topboots, and had apparently just come in from riding in the park.

"*Bonjour*, Mademoiselle," he smiled, his eye on the retreating Denise. "And how did the studies go today?"

"I'd like to have a word with you, monsieur," said Leonie, taking a sudden resolve.

"But of course. I'm quite at your disposal."

Leonie twisted her hands together nervously. "Monsieur, I think I should leave my post here," she said in a rush.

"But why? Has something happened? Has Denise—or one of the servants—been rude to you?"

"No, no, nothing like that at all. It's just that—you see, I don't feel that I'm helping Denise. She's simply not interested in learning, and nothing that I do seems to change her attitude. I don't like to take money unless I earn it, monsieur. Perhaps you should try another governess."

The comte laughed indulgently. "Come, now, I can see that you're blue-devilled about something—as my English friends would say—but I cannot allow your mood to influence your judgment. Not helping Denise? You're far too modest, I assure you. Since your arrival my niece has improved immeasurably. She has more grace, more gentility, and now she even knows that Molière is an author, not one of the tradesmen on Marylebone High Street! Please tell me that you've changed your mind, that you don't intend to leave us," he added with a coaxing smile.

Warmed by the comte's praise, Leonie allowed herself to be persuaded. "Very well, monsieur. I'll continue for at least a while longer."

"*Bon*. That's settled, then. And now, I have a little favour to ask of you."

"A favour? Why certainly. What can I do for you?"

"How kind of you. I'm giving a little dinner party on Saturday next, and I would like you to give my guests the pleasure of hearing you sing."

"I—I don't think that would be very wise," faltered Leonie. "I'm sure it would look very—very improper..."

"Ordinarily I would agree with you," said the comte, "especially in view of the fact that my little party will be for gentlemen only, since I have no hostess—for that I must wait, *vous comprenez*, for Denise's education to be completed. No, what I had in mind is something quite different: simply, that you come to the drawing room after dinner and entertain my guests very briefly until we turn to the main business of the evening, which, I must confess to you, will be a session at the card tables!"

Despite her misgivings, Leonie found herself responding to the comte's whimsical smile. "Very well, monsieur. I'll sing if you really wish me to."

Knowing Denise's jealous temperament as she did, Leonie was not surprised to discover that the girl resented the comte's proposal that Leonie sing at the dinner party. She was, however, surprised at the extent of the resentment. On the Saturday, as Leonie sat at her dressing table arranging her hair, she became increasingly annoyed at the sound of Denise's grumbling. The girl had come, unannounced and uninvited, to Leonie's room, throwing herself across the bed as she watched morosely while Leonie dressed.

"I still don't see why I can't come down with you," Denise remarked for the tenth time. "I'm as old as you are, and I'm also the comte's niece, more to the point."

"As I've told you, I'm not going down as a guest," Leonie replied, with as much patience as she could muster. "I will merely sing two songs, and then I'll return to my room. Your turn will come, Denise," she added placatingly. "As soon as you complete your education you'll be assuming your duties as your uncle's official hostess."

"But what harm can it do if I just go with you to the drawing room? I'd sit quietly and listen, I promise you—

perhaps I could even be helpful, turn your pages, something like that..."

"I'm sorry," said Leonie firmly as she prepared to leave the room. "Your uncle said specifically that you were not to come down. I simply can't go against his instructions."

As Leonie walked down the corridor past the dining room to the drawing room, she could hear the occasional burst of boisterous laughter, and wondered apprehensively if she would be facing a largely inebriated audience. In the drawing room she sat down at the pianoforte, playing softly and humming a few bars to open her throat. She was relieved, a little later, when the comte and his seven guests entered the drawing room, to observe that the gentlemen, though some of them were slightly flushed from the effects of their final bottle of port at the dinner table, did not appear more than marginally intoxicated.

"And now, gentlemen, if you will all sit down," began the comte, smiling brightly, "I should like to present to you a young lady who will delight you with her singing: Mademoiselle Leonie de Montbarey."

Flustered at singing before a group containing so many strangers, Leonie gradually gained confidence, losing herself in the music, until by the end of the second song, the same little Mozart aria that she had sung for the comte, she had almost forgotten that an audience was present.

As she finished her performance, she looked up, smiling shyly, and for the first time really looked at the occupants of the drawing room. Her heart skipped a beat as she saw, standing at the entrance of the room, leaning against the doorway with his arms folded against his chest, the tall figure of Jeremy Deveril.

As she rose, moving out from the pianoforte to drop a curtsey, the comte came forward, startling her by placing a familiar hand on her shoulder. "Please accept my gratitude, mademoiselle, and, I am sure, that of my guests also, for a charming performance. I hope that you will favour us with your singing many times in the future."

Murmuring her thanks, Leonie edged away from the comte's hand and hurried away from the drawing room. At the doorway she paused, smiling at Jeremy Deveril. "Mr. Deveril," she said, "how pleasant to see you again. I've been wanting to tell you how very much I appreciated the help you gave me in recommending Mrs. Kirby's house as a lodging."

Deveril inclined his head very slightly. His grey eyes were hard and his voice conveyed only icy indifference as he said, "Your thanks are quite unnecessary. It's obvious that you never required any help from anyone. You seem well able to help yourself." He gave her another bow of barest civility and moved away.

Leonie raced up the stairway, her eyes welling with tears as she tried to fathom the reason for Jeremy Deveril's seemingly deliberate hostility. Perhaps, she thought it was one thing to talk privately with a governess in the anonymity of a country inn, quite another to acknowledge her in the company of his peers. Wiping away her tears, she pushed open the door of her bedchamber, stopping short just over the threshold as she saw, with some surprise, that Denise was still in the room.

"Well, mademoiselle, did you have a tremendous triumph? And was my uncle the comte properly appreciative?"

Leonie looked at Denise narrowly. Even without the slurred speech and the bottle clutched in her hand as she lolled back against the bed, it would have been apparent that the girl had been drinking. The room reeked of gin.

"Denise," Leonie said, appalled, "how could you do such a thing? You're drunk!"

Denise sat up, brandishing the bottle. "Perhaps I am. And why not? Anyone who's been treated as I've been treated tonight deserves to have a little Blue Ruin to console herself."

Leonie walked over to the bed, reaching for the bottle. "Let me have that dreadful stuff. I'll dispose of it after I help you to your room and perhaps I can keep your uncle from finding out about this episode. I'm very much afraid, if he ever did discover that you'd actually been drinking gin, that he might change his plans to make you his official hostess."

Lurching away from Leonie's hand, Denise took another swig of gin, hiccupped loudly and said mournfully, "Don't be silly, mademoiselle. I'll never be the comte's hostess. He'll throw me out on the street, now that he's found a replacement for me. *You'll* be his hostess, just as you were tonight."

"What nonsense," Leonie gasped. "Of course, your uncle won't throw you out on the street! How can you even talk like that, after the comte has been so kind to you, searching for you all those years, taking you into his home as his niece even though there was no legal necessity for his doing so..."

"Oh, don't try to gammon me," sneered Denise. "Even a peagoose like you couldn't have been taken in by Uncle's story. You must have guessed that he's no more my uncle than I am the Princess of Wales."

"Well, of course, he's really your cousin, he uses the term *niece* merely as a convenience..."

Denise burst out laughing. "Come, now, my girl. You can't be as green as all that. Surely you must have realised that I'm his doxy. And that's what you'll be too, mademoiselle, before very much longer."

Leonie could feel the blood draining from her face. Her hands were clenched into trembling fists as she confronted Denise. "If this is your idea of a joke..."

"Oh, I'm not bamming you, *chérie*. I never laid eyes on the dear comte until about a year ago, when I was serving tables in my stepfather's cafe in Somers Town. I caught his attention and soon I had my own snug set of rooms and the use of a carriage and all the finery any girl could want. But of course, I was up to his rig when he told me that I was to come live in his house and pretend to be his niece while you taught me how to be a lady; I knew it was only a matter of time before he tried to turn you up sweet and persuade you to be his fancy piece in my place. There was nothing I could do about it, with the comte holding the purse strings, but when I met you I really thought at first that you might be the sweet ladylike creature you pretended to be, and perhaps the comte would get no place with you. But after our evening at the opera, with your wearing my clothes without so much as a by-my-leave—and don't think I missed that little by-play when he tenderly draped your shawl around your shoulders—and especially after tonight when I got pushed aside so that you could entertain his guests—well, even a ninny could see which way the wind was blowing.''

As she listened to Denise in horrified silence, Leonie thought back over the details of her relationship with the comte. She could see now that she had been deliberately blind, lest she endanger her position as governess, to the many signs of the comte's growing familiarity: his frequent visits to the classroom, his appreciative glances and overly fulsome praises, his lingering touch on her shoulder this evening. She could not doubt that both the visit to the opera and the request to sing to his guests were part of a well-orchestrated scheme to ease her gradually into appearing with him in public; after a few more such appearances it would be impossible for Leonie to convince anyone that her relationship with the comte was quite innocent. Her cheeks burned. Now she could understand the servants' very thinly veiled disdain for her, and the reason, too, for Jeremy Deveril's behaviour to her of a few minutes ago.

Leonie turned away from Denise, ripping off the lavender dress without regard to torn fabric and popping buttons. Throwing the dress on the floor she reached into the wardrobe for her own gown of sober jaconet muslin. She dressed quickly, and then, dragging her portmanteau from the bottom of the wardrobe, she began tossing her belongings into it.

Propping herself up on her elbow, Denise asked in alarm, "What are you doing?"

"That's obvious, isn't it? I'm packing my clothes, and when I finish I intend to leave this house. Immediately."

Denise scrambled out of the bed. "Oh, no, mademoiselle, you can't do that," she protested, suddenly sobered. "The comte will be so angry with me if he thinks I've driven you from the house. Please forget what I said. I was only funning. I say mad things when I've been drinking..."

"No, you weren't funning. You were finally saying exactly what you've been longing to say for weeks," snapped Leonie as she continued to throw her few belongings into her bag. It took only a few minutes to complete the packing, and then Leonie, donning her pelisse and tying the ribbons of her bonnet, picked up the portmanteau and strode purposefully from the room.

Behind her, Denise cried desperately, "No, no, I can't let you do this, you'll ruin everything—please come back." She dashed after Leonie, caterwauling ever more loudly, grabbing ineffectually at Leonie's arm as the latter began descending the stairway to the first floor.

By the time they reached the foyer Denise's wailing had reached such a pitch that the commotion brought the butler and several of his henchmen into the area.

"Is there anything amiss, mademoiselle?"

"Nothing at all, Mattson," said Leonie, staring down the butler's cold, unfriendly gaze. "I'm leaving the house. Please open the door."

"Don't let her go, Mattson. M. le Comte will have your head if you do," gabbled Denise.

"Will no one open the door?" demanded Leonie, eyeing

the group with a withering stare. "Well, it's no great matter. Step aside, please. I'll open it myself." She strode purposefully toward the door, only to have Denise sprint after her, catching her by the arm with another ear-piercing shriek of despair.

"Be quiet, you slut," exclaimed the butler, glancing behind him uneasily. "You'll disturb the master's guests. Now, mademoiselle, what am I to tell M. le Comte about your decision to leave this house in the middle of the night?"

"I'm under no necessity to explain anything to you," gritted Leonie. "I'm just going, that's all." She turned back to the door just as the comte, his brows drawn together in a forbidding scowl, entered the foyer. "What is the meaning of this unseemly noise?" he demanded of the butler.

"I'm very sorry, M. le Comte. I fear that there's some kind of misunderstanding. Mlle. de Montbarey tells me that she is leaving the house immediately, and Mlle. de Tonneville is objecting strenuously."

"Is this true, mademoiselle? you wish to leave us?" The comte's scowl was replaced by a look of pained surprise. "Don't you think that you at least owe me the courtesy of explaining the reason for this—ah—very sudden departure?"

"I don't care to go into my reasons," Leonie said coldly. "I suggest that you ask Denise."

The latter erupted into a howl of fear. "Please don't be angry with me, monsieur. I didn't mean any harm, truly."

Ignoring his "niece," the comte assured Leonie, switching from the English he had been using to the servants to French, "There has obviously been a terrible misunderstanding. If you will just wait until the morning, I feel sure that I can explain everything to your satisfaction." To Denise, he said contemptuously, "Get upstairs. I'll settle affairs with you when you've sobered up."

As Denise, sobbing wildly, worked herself into a fit of

screaming hysterics, Leonie said, "No, I won't stay, monsieur. There is no possible explanation for your actions."

"Now wait," said the comte, walking over to her and laying a placating hand on her arm, "I don't doubt that Denise has been telling you some kind of lying story, but you see the state she's in, surely you can't believe a word that she says..."

Leonie jerked away from him. "It's you who's been telling lies, M. le Comte. You installed your mistress in this house as your 'niece,' and hired me to act as her governess until such time as you could seduce me and make Denise's masquerade unnecessary."

"No, no, you are completely wrong about this—if you will only let me explain..." The comte broke off as Jeremy Deveril moved forward from the rear of the foyer. "Ah, there Mr Deveril," he said in English, "please let me apologise for this disturbance. A domestic matter, you will understand, I am sure."

Deveril walked over to Leonie's side. "Mlle. de Montbarey you seem to be in difficulty. Can I help you in any way?"

"No, thank you, Mr. Deveril, your assistance is the very last thing in the world I want," said Leonie icily. "I bid you a good night, sir." She wrenched open the door, picked up her bag and hurried down the steps. It was a very dark night without moon or stars, and as she walked past the line of waiting carriages belonging to the comte's guests, her heart began to sink at the thought of walking, alone and in the dead of night, all the way to Mrs. Kirby's pastry shop. But the alternative was to return to the comte's house and put herself once again in his power, she told herself, hurrying her steps and devoutly hoping that she was going in the right direction. After a few moments she heard footsteps behind her and Jeremy Deveril's voice calling to her. Ignoring the call she walked even faster, but soon he loomed up beside her as she reached the gaslight at the corner of the street.

"Please stop, Mlle. de Montbarey, I'd like to speak to you for a moment."

"We have nothing to say to each other," said Leonie, continuing to walk.

"I'll only keep you a moment," said Deveril, placing a restraining hand on her arm. Leonie whirled around, looking up into his handsome, arrogant face under the curling beaver hat as she cried angrily, "Please go away, Mr. Deveril. Or must I complain to the watch that you're molesting me?"

"Believe me, I have no thought of molesting you. But surely you must realise that it's not safe for a young woman to be walking around London by herself in the middle of the night. Won't you let me help you?"

The calm superiority of his tone nettled Leonie. "I don't want your help," she flashed. "As you remarked earlier this evening, I'm well able to help myself."

Swiftly he answered, "Forgive me for saying that. I see now that I was completely wrong in my estimate of your situation."

Leonie bit her lip, fighting for control. The unexpected sympathy in his voice took the edge off the anger and indignation that had fuelled her headlong flight from the comte's house. She said in a small voice, "I accept your apology, but there is no reason for you to concern yourself further with my affairs."

Again taking her arm, Deveril said, kindly and reasonably, "I of course will not interfere in your affairs if you don't wish me to, but won't you at least allow me to escort you in my carriage to your destination?"

Leonie hesitated, glancing around her at the dark, deserted street. Then, swallowing her pride, she said, "Thank you. Would you take me to Mrs. Kirby's lodging, please?"

In the carriage, somewhat crowded because of the necessity of stowing Leonie's baggage inside, there was silence for some minutes until Deveril said quietly, "I don't wish to embarrass you, but am I correct in assuming that you came to the Comte de Morville's house under the impression that you were to teach his niece? I speak some French, you see, and I was standing at the rear of the foyer for some minutes before I spoke to you."

Leonie felt her face flaming in the darkness. "Yes," she said reluctantly.

"And I gather also, from the 'niece's' drunken blubbering, that you discovered the truth only this evening, after you sang for us in the drawing room."

"How could I have been so stupid as to believe such a cock-and-bull story?" cried Leonie, her constraint suddenly swept away. The words came in torrents. "You see, the comte told me that Denise had become separated from her mother in the Low Countries after the defeat of the Princes' army, and that he had only just located her, after she had been reared by a family of humble artisans. I believed that her commonness, her vulgarity, were the result of her upbringing, because I knew how difficult life was for so many of the émigrés. I met the comte at the home of my parents' friend, the Comtesse de Vaucouleurs, and he had known my parents, too, and I—I really thought that he was just being kind. . ." Leonie gulped, taking hard, deep breaths as she brushed away the silent tears.

Deveril reached across to place a folded handkerchief in Leonie's hands. "Put it all behind you," he said kindly. "You couldn't have known that the comte had a reputation for collecting high-flyers. He simply made a mistake in judgement about you."

But Leonie, resting her head against the squabs of the carriage, wondered silently if the comte had been moved to attempt to take advantage of her because of his knowledge of her clouded parentage. She felt certain that the daughter, or the niece, or the sister of any of the comte's émigré friends, regardless of the present economic circumstances of her family, would have been quite safe from his roving eye.

"Perhaps it would be of some comfort for you to know that I, too, made a bad mistake in judgement," Deveril said after a moment. "When I saw you in Morville's company at the opera the other night, I assumed that you had become his latest conquest. So when, several days later, I met him at Angelo's, I accepted his dinner invitation. I am only slightly acquainted with the comte, and frankly, I would prefer to keep it that way—the man's reputation at the tables has long been suspect. But—forgive me—I went to his house because I wished to verify my suspicions of you. And when you appeared to sing for us, I concluded that my suspicions were correct."

"Don't apologise to me," said Leonie with a sigh. "Anyone would have thought the same in your place."

The carriage stopped, and Leonie, glancing out, saw that they had arrived at the darkened pastry shop. "What will Mrs. Kirby think of me, arriving at her home at such an hour?" she asked in sudden dismay. "Perhaps I should go to an hotel instead."

"My dear girl, I can assure you that it would look even odder for a single, unaccompanied young woman to ask for a room in any good London hotel at this time of night," replied Deveril drily. "Let me talk to Mrs. Kirby. I think you'll find that she'll make no difficulties at all."

Such proved to be the case. After a considerable delay and much discreet knocking, Mrs. Kirby finally appeared at her door, owlish and plainly disapproving at the sight of her former lodger, back on her doorstep under such out-of-the-way circumstances. But it took Jeremy Deveril only a few moments, with his winning smile and an affectionate hand on her shoulder, to bring the ex-housekeeper around. Indeed, when Deveril sketched for her the tale of the comte's evil design on a helpless Leonie, Mrs. Kirby became her outraged champion. "That man did ought to be punished, Miss Leonie," she said roundly. "We ought to have him up before the magistrate for kidnapping, or some such thing."

"No doubt the villain richly deserves it, but we can't have Mademoiselle embarrassed, now, can we, Mrs. K.?" Deveril cajoled her. Turning to Leonie, he bowed, saying, "I hope that you can put all this unpleasantness out of your mind. I think you'll find that problems have a way of looking better in the morning. Good night, and sleep well."

After she had fallen into bed exhausted, shepherded there by a briskly maternal Mrs. Kirby, Leonie found it difficult to drift off to sleep. Her mind kept returning to the machinations of the Comte de Morville, and despite her relief at having escaped unscathed from the house on Mount Street, she felt a growing chagrin at how easily she had been duped. She knew that she ought to be grateful to Jeremy Deveril—looking back, she now realised that without his timely appearance on the scene the comte might have used physical force to prevent her leaving—but instead she was filled with a quite illogical resentment at the high-handed arrogance that had characterised his handling of the situation from the first to last, as if she were a small child whose life must be completely arranged for her.

5

"I'M SORRY, MISS Leonie, I couldn't keep him out, he just brushed right by me," said Mrs. Kirby, her plump, smooth face twisted by a worried frown.

Leonie looked up in surprise as she sat reading her newspaper. There in the doorway of the parlour, behind Mrs. Kirby's stout form, loomed the tall, elegant figure of the Comte de Morville.

It was a week since Leonie's hasty departure from the comte's house, and she had hoped fervently that she would never see him again. Several days previously, returning from another fruitless visit to the Labour Exchange, Leonie had been informed by Mrs. Kirby that the comte had called to see her. "If he should come again, tell him that I am not at home to him," Leonie had instructed Mrs. Kirby. The faithful landlady had indeed turned away the comte on each of the succeeding days until today, when, apparently, his patience had run out.

"What do you want me to do, Miss Leonie?" asked Mrs.

Kirby with an apprehensive glance behind her. "Shall I fetch Kirby to throw him out?"

"No, no, don't do that," said Leonie hastily at the very thought of calling upon Mrs. Kirby's elderly, near-sighted husband to be her champion. She rose, drawing herself up to her full height. "Perhaps you didn't understand the message Mrs. Kirby gave you, M. le Comte," she said levelly. "If so, I will repeat it. I do not wish to see you and I ask you to leave immediately."

Giving the affronted landlady a gentle shove, the comte edged past her into the parlour. "If you will give me just five minutes of your time, I promise to leave the house without any further prompting," he said pleasantly, but firmly.

Leonie hesitated. Five minutes of conversation seemed little enough to ensure that she would never have to see the man again. "Very well," she said at last. "Five minutes only. Mrs. Kirby, you may leave. I shall be quite all right."

After the landlady's departure, the comte stripped off his gloves, placing them inside his beaver hat, which he deposited on a small table near the door. "I may sit down?" he smiled.

"I prefer to stand, monsieur," said Leonie briefly.

"As you will," shrugged the comte. "You have little cause to be friendly with me, heaven knows. Mademoiselle, I'll come right to the point: please allow me to apologise for the distressing events that caused you to leave my house so hastily the other evening. Denise had no right to inflict her drunken babbling upon you."

"Are you saying that Denise was lying?"

"Well, not telling the entire truth, at any rate," replied the comte easily. "She's not my niece, of course. And yes, I did install her as my mistress for a time. But it is not true, as she insinuated, that I intended to trick you, to force you in some way to become her successor."

Leonie lifted her chin. "You wish me to believe that your only object in employing me was to improve Denise's mind? After I had, somehow, changed her into a cultured lady, you were planning to send me on my way with your gratitude and an enthusiastic letter of reference?"

"Now you're being sarcastic, *bien entendu*," said the comte with a look of pained amusement. "I can scarcely blame you. No, I freely admit that I had no real interest in your educating Denise—though you performed miracles with her in the short time you worked with her and it can only be of profit for her in any future liaison. What I hoped would happen was that you would gradually become aware of how much I admired you, and that, at some future time, you would agree to live under my protection. Not as my mistress of the moment, like poor Denise. I had in mind a more permanent arrangement: your own house, your own carriage, and a substantial settlement. If and when we parted company, you would never again need to worry about your future. So you can see that your suspicions—that I intended your forced seduction or perish the thought, even rape—were entirely unfounded."

Leonie stared at him incredulously. His complacent smile and reasonable tone indicated clearly that he considered it highly likely that she would accept his proposal once she realised the generosity of his offer. "Please leave," she exclaimed in a voice choked with rage. "You have now insulted me more thoroughly than you succeeded in doing the other evening. There can be nothing more that you could possibly say to me."

The comte's eyes narrowed. "Now, just a moment, my girl. In what, pray, lies the insult in offering a great position and even luxury to a poverty-stricken little nobody?"

"I would remind you that I am not a nobody—you met me in the home of an eminently respectable friend, you knew my parents personally..."

"I knew the Baron and Baronne de Montbarey," replied the comte pointedly. "But they were not your parents, *n'est-ce pas?* They rescued a nameless infant in a low Dutch boarding house, and because Mme. de Montbarey was childless they decided to adopt the baby. They knew nothing at all about your antecedents—you could be the child of a scullery maid, or an escaped murderess. No one knows, nor will ever know. I'm personally grateful that the Montbareys reared you as the daughter of their house because I infinitely prefer the company of a cultivated, well-bred woman as my mistress to that of vulgar little Denise. But you mistake yourself badly if you think that, with your clouded parentage, you would ever be accepted socially in any circle other than the demimonde."

As she listened to the comte's cruelly wounding words, Leonie could feel her heart constricting again with the secret anguish she had been experiencing ever since she had read her foster father's revealing letter. She clenched her hands into fists to control their trembling, striving to keep her voice contained as she said, "I refuse to listen to any more of this, monsieur. If you won't leave, I shall. Mrs. Kirby will show you out." She turned on her heel and made for the door, gasping as the comte seized her, his fingers biting hard into her shoulders."

"Enchanting little vixen," he smiled down at her. "You're more than beautiful—you have fire and spirit and I'm enslaved by you. I must have you, chérie. Name your own price, but I must have you." He bent his head to bury his face in her throat while his eager fumbling fingers clawed at the collar of her gown.

Her arms and legs flailing, Leonie was struggling fiercely to release herself when suddenly the comte's grasp relaxed and he staggered backwards across the floor to land in a heap against the wall. Leonie looked up, panting, to find Jeremy Deveril standing between herself and the comte with an apprehensive Mrs. Kirby in the background.

"Mr. Jeremy just arrived, Miss Leonie. I thought perhaps I had better send him in here."

Jeremy Deveril, straightening his neckcloth and smoothing a lock of hair that had fallen over his forehead, said politely, "I am correct, am I not, mademoiselle, in assuming that you did not welcome the comte's advances?"

"Oh, yes, yes," shuddered Leonie. "Please make him go, Mr. Deveril."

"You heard the young lady, Morville," said Deveril to the comte, who was walking slowly to the center of the room, massaging his chin, which was rapidly turning red and swollen. "Will you leave voluntarily, or must I assist you?"

"You hit me, Deveril," said the comte venomously. "You'll meet me for this." He picked up his hat from the table near the door, turning to address Deveril. "My second will be contacting you."

Deveril sighed. "As you wish. Of course, duels are now illegal in England, and they are really beginning to seem rather old hat to the Ton—but I'm quite willing to oblige you, especially if it will be a warning to you in the future to refrain from attempting to seduce girls of good family. I collect that I, as the challenged party, have the choice of weapons?" He looked thoughtfully at the comte. "Pistols, I think. I believe you've seen me shoot at Manton's Galleries."

The comte glared at Deveril, almost audibly grinding his teeth. "My compliments. You've won this round," he spat out. "No doubt it flatters your vanity to pose as the champion of the innocent. But I fancy that you'll be sorry one day, when you discover that this 'young girl of good family' belongs in the gutter where I found her. Reaching out blindly, he shoved Mrs. Kirby from his path and left the room.

Her face flaming at the comte's malevolent insinuations, Leonie turned away. "Thank you for coming to my rescue, Mr. Deveril," she said in a strangled voice.

"Not at all. My pleasure," Deveril assured her politely. "I would have hit him a little harder if I had anticipated the kind of poison he was about to spew out. Mrs. Kirby, could you bring us some tea? This has been an unsettling experience for Mademoiselle." He put his hand under Leonie's arm, guiding her gently to a chair. "Don't dwell on what Morville said," he advised her. "He was furious enough to say anything that came into his head, including that flight of the imagination about finding you in a gutter. Though, I must say, it's hard to imagine what even a man of his venom could have meant to convey by that remark. I thought that he met you at the home of his friend the Comtesse de Vaucouleurs."

Her face suffused with colour, Leonie answered in a low voice without lifting her head. "He was referring to the fact that I'm an adopted child," she said reluctantly. She gave Deveril a brief account of the story that she herself had so recently learned from her father's last letter. "I can see now that I was very stupid, or naive, or both, not to have realised from the first what the comte's intentions really were. The tale he told me about Denise's origins was far too much like my own to be a coincidence; I should have seen it for what it was, a ruse to gain my confidence and lull my suspicions to the point where I would fall into his hands like a ripe plum," she finished bitterly.

"I see. Well, I should put it all behind me if I were you. You're not likely to see anything more of the Comte de Morville. Ah, here's the tea. And I see that you're catering to my weakness, Mrs. K."

"As if I could forget that those little cakes were your favorites, Mr. Jeremy," said Mrs. Kirby, eyeing him with doting fondness. "Do enjoy your tea, now, and ring if you want anything else."

Deveril smiled after her retreating figure. "Her bump of curiosity about the villainous Comte de Morville is almost lifting the cap off her head," he remarked indulgently. "Will you do the honours? I like just a scant teaspoon of sugar."

But Leonie, ignoring the tea, asked anxiously, "Will you really be forced to fight a duel with the comte? I don't think that I could bear it if any harm came to you on my account."

Deveril raised an eyebrow. "Thank you for your solicitude, but I assure you that I'm in no danger of injury from Morville in a duel. The man's a ludicrously poor shot. No, I fancy that I've heard the last of any challenge from that quarter."

Later, after Leonie had drunk a calming cup of tea, Deveril said, "Might I inquire if you have found a new position?"

"No. I've answered several advertisements, and I've had one interview at the Labour Exchange, since—since I left the Comte de Morville. But I've had no offer of a position."

"Then I should like to offer you one. As the governess to my sister's daughters. In a recent letter Caroline mentioned that the governess was leaving and that another would have to be found. So I wrote to her just under a week ago, suggesting you for the post. She replied yesterday, accepting my suggestion with considerable gratitude. If you like, I can drive you down to Granby Court tomorrow."

Leonie looked at him, her eyes wide with surprise. "I—I couldn't possibly accept your offer," she stammered.

"Oh—and why not? I though you were actively looking for a position, and I can assure you that my sister's household is eminently respectable."

"Now you're teasing me, Mr. Deveril. It's just that—you see—well, your sister has not even met me," Leonie floundered.

"But then, you're not likely to have met any other prospective employer either, isn't that correct?" he asked with lifted eyebrow.

"Yes, but—Mr. Deveril, I thank you very much, but you must see that I am already so much indebted to you, I simply can't allow you to do anything more for me."

To Leonie's chagrin, Deveril's face assumed the rather bored, superior expression that had nettled her on several previous occasions. "Come now, aren't you being rather foolish? Biting off your nose to spite your face?" He lifted a commanding hand to forestall Leonie's burst of indignation. Continuing in the same calm, reasonable tones—as if he were speaking to a fractious child, Leonie thought resentfully— Deveril said, "Rather than your being indebted to me, I can assure you that the shoe would be on the other foot. My sister, Lady Ashbury, has found it virtually impossible to keep a governess because her children are close to being unmanageable. I won't go into boring family history, but I must tell you that Caroline has had a difficult life—the births of ten children have left her in delicate health and there have been family problems—" He paused as he noted Leonie's sudden look of understanding. "I see that Mrs. Kirby has been indulging in her favorite pastime, gossiping about the Deverils," he said drily. "Well, then, to go on: the children are quite likeable, actually, but they are high-spirited and fond of an active country life, and their governesses have found it impossible to control them without some discipline from Caroline, which they don't receive. The children have always been able to wind my sister around their little fingers."

Interested in spite of herself, Leonie asked, "I'm wondering why you think that I would be a good candidate for this difficult post, Mr. Deveril?"

"Well, I noticed, in your account of your experiences with Morville's—er, ward—that you seemed to have some liking for the girl, and some sympathy for her, despite her unpromising personality and aversion to learning. And I gather that you were able to teach her something, were you not? So I think we can assume that you are a natural teacher. And then, in thinking back on the parade of governesses that have come and gone in my sister's household, I realised that they were all middle-aged. Perhaps it's time to see what a young person can do with my strong-willed nieces. So what about it, mademoiselle? Will you give the post a try? Say, for six months—if, at the end of that time you and Lady Ashbury find that you don't suit, why, neither of you has lost anything."

After a long pause, Leonie said quietly, "Thank you. I accept the position."

"That's settled then," said Deveril, rising. "I'll come by for you at eight tomorrow morning. Granby Court is something over one hundred miles from London, and we can make the journey in eight or nine hours if you don't become overly fatigued."

Deveril, clad in buckskin breeches and a many-caped driving coat, arrived prompt to the minute next morning, in a hired post chaise behind four horses, with two postillions. They headed north on the "New Road," past the fields and farmlands surrounding the newly-built-up areas of Somers Town and Pentonville, and across Finchley Common—where, Deveril informed her, his father had once been a victim of one of the hordes of highwaymen who formerly preyed on travellers in the area—to the first stage stop at Barnet. Leonie soon discovered that there was a vast difference between travelling by stagecoach and private chaise. There was the matter of speed—in the chaise they hurtled along, so Deveril told her, at a rather frightening eleven or twelve miles an hour. Then there was the service: alerted by the post-boy blowing his horn for the "change" as the chaise approached the inn, the hostlers at the Green Man in Barnet were already waiting in the courtyard when the chaise rolled through the gate; within five minutes they had changed the teams and the chaise was out of the courtyard and off on its journey via the Great North Road. The routine varied slightly at some of the posting inns, at all of which, Leonie noted, Deveril was apparently well known to the deferential staffs: at the Swann Inn in Stevenage, 31 miles from London, they stopped for coffee and pastries, and at Huntington, in early afternoon, they paused to "bait" on cold meat, cake and fruit.

During the course of the long day, Leonie learned a great deal about the family of her future employer. Of Lady Ashbury's ten children, the eldest, Fanny, had been married the year before to Lord Durrington. John, the new Marquis of Ashbury, was at Cambridge, as was Thomas, soon to go into the army; his twin, Lydia, would come out the following spring. Edward and William were at Harrow, George was still in knee breeches, and Amabel, Charlotte and Augusta would be Leonie's charges in the schoolroom.

"You needn't try to keep them all sorted out from the very beginning," Deveril advised her carelessly. "You'll doubtless meet them all at Christmas time, but for the present you'll be dealing only with the schoolroom contingent. And Lydia, of course. I'm going to advise Caroline that Lydia should come to you to have her French polished."

In the afternoon, as they crossed into Lincolnshire, Leonie was intrigued by her first glimpse of the great flat fen country, different from the rolling downs around Winchester with which she was so familiar. "Ages ago all this area was a vast swamp," Deveril told her, "but now it is so well drained that it is one of the best agricultural regions in England. The drainage system goes all the way back to the Romans." Leonie reflected, smiling reminiscently, how much her father, with his keen scholarly mind, would have been interested in Deveril's remarks.

At Grantham they turned off the Great North Road at last, and soon the chaise was starting up a long, curving driveway edged with trees, with occasional glimpses of deer grazing in the open spaces of a great park, and, in the distance, a small, artfully "ruined" Greek temple. As they rounded the last curve of the driveway, a large house came into view, a vast structure with a great pillared portico and sweeping wings attached to the main block by curving corridors. "How beautiful," breathed Leonie; "it looks exactly like the designs by Palladio that my father admired so much."

"Yes, the house was built to a design by Palladio by the late marquis's grandfather when he returned from his Grand Tour," said Deveril. "It cost a great deal to build, of course; it was the beginning of the decline of the family fortunes. Though, I must say, my late brother-in-law did his best to accelerate that decline."

Even before the chaise had come to a stop in front of the portico, several liveried servants had assembled on the steps.

"Afternoon, Chesley," said Deveril to the butler as he lifted his hand to Leonie to assist her from the carriage. "Please escort Mlle. de Montbarey to the morning room and inform her ladyship that we've arrived, while I see to the post-boys."

Feeling a slight twinge of nervousness at the unexpected grandeur of Granby Court, Leonie followed the butler through a marble-floored entrance hall to a small salon panelled in a pale damask satin and furnished with graceful satinwood furniture; on the ceiling delicate moldings separated the surface into small compartments painted with colourful scenes of dancing nymphs and fantastic legendary beasts.

Leonie had waited only a few minutes when Lady Ashbury entered the room. The marchioness was a slight woman with a pretty, worn face and fair hair sprinkled with grey tucked under a becoming lace cap. The gentle voice and tired blue eyes were warm and welcoming as she extended her hand to Leonie.

"I am so happy to meet you, my dear. My brother has quite whetted our curiosity about you! Do sit down and tell me about your journey. You left London only this morning? How monstrous! That brother of mine has absolutely no regard for female sensibilities. You must be quite exhausted. There you are, Jeremy," she said, smiling affectionately as her brother entered the salon and bent over to drop a kiss on her forehead. "Be warned—I'm going to chide you for inflicting such a wearying journey on this poor child. How much better if you had broken the drive halfway."

"You can see for yourself, Caro, that Mademoiselle seems to have survived the journey remarkably well," grinned Deveril. "And I'll confess, I'm somewhat pressed for time. I must return to town tomorrow. And so, Caro, how is the family? How is Ashbury doing at Cambridge?"

"Oh, well, Jeremy, you know John is no great scholar. He writes that he's anxious to come home to start managing the estate."

"There's no great hurry for him to come home," said Deveril carelessly. "Let him stay up at Cambridge for a while, learn a little something. Your new steward Martin can handle the estate very well until John is ripe for responsibility."

"I daresay you're right," said Lady Ashbury, with what Leonie suspected was just a touch too much submissiveness to her younger brother.

"And how is Lydia?" asked Deveril with a smile. "Chafing at the bit, if I know her, until she comes out next spring."

"You know our Lydia all too well," replied Lady Ashbury, returning his smile. "Oh, I must tell you, Jeremy, we've just heard—Fanny is increasing."

"Good God, Caro, you're much too young to be a grandmother."

"Not at all," said Caroline drawing herself up. "I'm quite looking forward to having a grandchild. Haven't you noticed, my hair is becoming quite grey." She turned her attention to Leonie. "My dear child, I'm convinced that you must be very tired." She rang the bell. 'I think that you should go to your room now and rest. The maids will bring you a tray whenever you ring."

"I'll say good-bye now, mademoiselle," said Deveril. "I'll be off for London very early in the morning. I wish you the greatest of luck with the children. Just be sure you keep a firm upper hand over them..."

"Jeremy!" said Lady Ashbury reproachfully. "I hope that you haven't given Mademoiselle the wrong idea about the girls. Of course, I know that they're high-spirited, but all that they need is the proper guidance, which I'm sure Mademoiselle will be able to give..."

"What those daughters of yours need, Caro, is discipline," retorted Deveril bluntly. "Quite frankly, if they're allowed to go on as they have, you'll have a pack of hoydens on your hands. And mind, I think it essential that Lydia, too, sits in with mademoiselle, at least part of the time, to polish her French and her music."

"Oh, dear, Lydia won't like that."

"Make her do it anyway. It will be good for her."

As Leonie followed the footman up the sweeping curve of the divided staircase, she wondered if Lady Ashbury ever resented what appeared to be the practically total control that her brother exercised over her family.

The room that Leonie had been assigned was spacious and prettily furnished, even more attractive and comfortable than the bedchamber she had occupied in the Comte de Morville's house. After eating the delicious hot supper that the maid brought up, she undressed and sank into the great four-poster bed, drowsy after the long tiring day but unable to relax completely as she thought about this new chapter in her life that had just begun.

6

"*Je viens, tu viens, il vient, nous venons, vouz venez, ils viennent.*"

"That was excellent, Amabel."

"But mademoiselle, I know I'll forget the conjugation by tomorrow," said Amabel despairingly. "And besides, I sound so terrible, so—so *English*!"

"Nonsense, Amabel. You're progressing beautifully. I'm proud of you."

Leonie looked at the serious, attentive young faces and reflected on how much the situation had changed since she had first confronted the three girls, on the day after her arrival at Granby Court, three months before. She glanced out into the bare landscape of the park, sombre in the austere mid-November light—yes, it really was that long ago. Then, on that first day, the three faces were wary, noncommittal. Leonie had known, as well as if the girls had openly expressed their hostility, that she was about to be tested. She had talked with them about what they had already studied, and came to the depressing conclusion that they had not studied very much. Queried about their favorite subject, the girls had exclaimed unanimously that they didn't have any—they much preferred outdoor amusements, especially riding, to classes.

"Do you ride a great deal?" Leonie had asked, and when they replied, "Oh, yes, Miss Goode let us go off to the stables every day after lunch, sometimes before lunch," Leonie took her first step toward establishing her authority over the classroom. "From now on," she told the girls firmly, "there will be no riding nor outdoor activity of any kind, on any day that you haven't worked hard in the classroom." There had been a great outcry, of course, and Amabel, always the ringleader, had cried hotly, "Mama won't approve of that, I assure you, mademoiselle." But Lady Ashbury had approved, and by now, though the Marlowe girls would never be scholars, they were at least resigned to being educated. Leonie had caught their interest initially by relating their studies to their passion for horses: arithmetic was bearable if one could use it to compute the speed or the weight of a favorite mare; the globes became fascinating when Leonie explained how the ancestors of the English thoroughbred had come from Arabia. English history ceased to be dry as dust because of Leonie's knack of making the Black Prince or King Alfred come alive in story vignettes, and French history was brought down to a personal level when Leonie related the tale of her family's spine-tingling escape from the Low Countries.

Leonie's thoughts were brought back to the present as an entrancingly pretty girl burst into the room. Lady Lydia Marlowe, seventeen years old, dimpled, with short flyaway curls, much resembled her three younger sisters, though Amabel, Augusta and Charlotte were still rather awkward and coltish, and Augusta was positively plump. But they were all very pretty, with light-brown hair, bright blue eyes and fine teeth and a strong resemblance to Lady Ashbury as she must have looked in her youth. "Sorry to be late, mademoiselle," gasped Lydia.

"Do try to be on time, please. Have you prepared the reading from Montesquieu?"

"*Il est vrai dans les démocraties, le peuple parait faire ce qu'il veut...*" began Lydia obediently.

"*Bon.* Your accent is improving. For the next class, I think that you'll enjoy a poem by François Villon." And when Lydia thanked her governess, and even said that she was looking forward to a stint of French poetry, Leonie realized that she had come very far indeed. For Lydia, on that first day at Granby Court, had proved to be a very difficult case. She had come into the classroom sullen and unwilling, protesting that it was unfair to make her into a schoolgirl again when she was about to come out in the spring. Leonie, giving her a long, measuring look, had asked politely, "And what are your expectations in coming out?"

"Why, to make a good marriage, of course."

"I see. You know, there are so many girls coming out each year, I fancy that most of them find it very hard to be noticed in such a crowd. Don't you think you would stand a better chance of finding a really eligible husband if you spoke good French and Italian, and if you played the piano well and sang a little?" The question had caught the impressionable Lydia's attention, and marked the beginning of her conquest. Leonie soon realised that the girl was lonely; she had been very close to her older sister Fanny and considered herself far too grown-up to associate with the three younger girls. And Lydia was a romantic, revelling in the Gothic novels of Monk Lewis and Mrs. Radcliffe. She found the stories of her governess's adventurous early life irresistibly intriguing and spent hours speculating about Leonie's return to France to discover her ancestry, once that ogre Bonaparte had been defeated.

Lydia had, in fact, come to look upon Leonie as a wiser, older sister in place of the married Fanny, and Leonie sometimes wondered uneasily if the relationship had not, in fact, become too close. For Lydia, who often came to Leonie's room late at night to exchange confidences, was an inveterate prattler, pouring out details of family gossip to which Leonie was very sure she should not be privy.

In the course of Lydia's artless disclosures, Leonie learned that John, the new marquis and oldest brother, had begun to gamble so extravagantly during his first year at Cambridge that his poor mama was nearly frantic with worry that he would be just like his papa; but, fortunately, Uncle Jeremy had soon straightened John out by warning him that he, Jeremy, would see his nephew blackballed at White's and Watier's, London's most exclusive clubs, unless John mended his ways.

Lydia was also an inexhaustible fount of information about Jeremy Deveril, who, it appeared, was a much sought-after catch by anxious London mamas since he had become his great-uncle's heir. But, said Lydia, with her usual zest for the romantic, Uncle Jeremy showed little inclination to settle down and get married, doubtless because he still kept alive the flame of his earlier, youthful romance with one Selena Cartwright; at the time, Deveril was a poor matrimonial prospect, since his elder brother was still alive, and Selena's father had arranged her marriage to a wealthy and titled suitor. "And the very next year Mama's older brother died and Uncle Jeremy was suddenly a very eligible bachelor, but it was too late, Selena was married to Lord Chudleigh," Lydia had mourned.

Many of Lydia's stories revolved around the shadowy but all powerful figure of Great Uncle Leonard, Earl of Winchcombe. "Only, of course, he's not really our uncle. Let me see now, the earl's father and our grandfather were first cousins, but

Uncle Leonard was an only child and he has no children of his own—his wife died many years ago and he never remarried—so now the line comes down through our branch of the family. Uncle Jeremy would come into the title in any event, but Mama says that he will also inherit the earl's immense personal fortune—when Uncle was young he went out with the East India Company and was immensely successful. Fanny says—that's my married sister, you know, Lady Durrington—that Uncle Jeremy will be one of the wealthiest men in England some day. Unless of course Uncle Jeremy and the old earl have a falling out; then the earl might leave away from Uncle Jeremy all but the entailed portion of the estate. But that's not very likely to happen, they rub along together very well."

More and more it seemed to Leonie that the Earl of Winchcombe was the magnet around which the affairs of the Marlowe family revolved. According to Lydia he was a recluse who rarely ventured away from his great estates, but his influence was all-pervasive, especially since Lady Ashbury had found herself in such a precarious financial situation following the death of her gambler husband. Lydia was sure that the earl had provided the money for her sister Fanny's dowry, and he had promised to buy commissions in the army and the navy for both Thomas and Edward and to provide a good living for William if the boy showed any inclination for the church. And, to the younger children's delight, the earl was the source of handsome money gifts at Christmas and on their birthdays.

"Guess what? Uncle Jeremy's coming here for Christmas, and Mama says that we may send out invitations for a small dance during his visit."

The squeal of joy occasioned by Lord Thomas Marlowe's statement roused Leonie from a reverie. She stared severely at the tall, handsome young man, very much the would-be dandy in his skin-tight buckskin breeches, high shirt points and extravagantly careless Belcher neckerchief. He had arrived home some weeks before, sent down from Cambridge because of an incident involving—so Lydia hinted—a boisterous party that had ended in an attempt to box the watch. He was staying at Granby Court while he awaited the arrival of his army commission. "You know that you shouldn't disrupt us while we're having lessons, Thomas," Leonie scolded.

"I'm sorry, mademoiselle, I won't do it again. Am I forgiven?" replied Thomas, his contrite tone belied by an impish grin to which Leonie found it hard not to respond. It would have been difficult, indeed, not to respond to the insouciant charm that Thomas shared with his siblings, but in the early days of his arrival from Cambridge he had proved no exception to the rule that the Marlowe children required special handling. For Thomas, newly arrived at the status of man-about-town, had been instantly smitten with his family's new governess. After an attempt to put his arm around her waist resulted in a vigorous box on the ear, however, Thomas and Leonie became good friends.

"Are you sure that Uncle Jeremy is coming here at Christmas, Thomas?" asked Lydia. "He usually comes at some time during the holidays, but last year, you'll remember, he arrived after the New Year. Uncle Jeremy has so many invitations to the best houses, you know, Chatworth and Belvoir and I don't know how many others," she explained to Leonie. She knitted her brow. "I know! she said suddenly. "Just the other day Henrietta Cartwright told me that her sister Selena would be visiting her parents at Christmastime. *That's* why Uncle Jeremy is arriving so early."

"That will be enough gossip, Lydia," said Leonie with a quelling look.

"Lord, mademoiselle, there's nothing to that," said Thomas

good-naturedly. "Everybody knows that Uncle Jeremy used to be sweet on Selena Cartwright. All right, all right," he exclaimed, as Leonie's expression became even more severe. "I really came to ask you if we could arrange another practice dancing session, since Mama says that we may have a small ball—a very small ball," he added conscientiously.

"Oh, yes, mademoiselle, please say that you'll play for us," begged Lydia. "I need—oh, so much extra practice."

"You have it all wrong, Lydia," said Thomas firmly. "*You* will play for us and mademoiselle will dance with me. She's a far better dancer than any of you."

"Don't talk fustian, Thomas," said Leonie, but inwardly she felt a small glow of pleasure, because, while playing the pianoforte during the girls' recent lessons with the dancing master, she had found herself picking up the steps and had practiced them surreptitiously in her bedchamber. And last week, when Thomas had been unable to grasp a certain figure in the country dance, only Leonie could untangle his feet. She was not deceiving herself, of course. It was unlikely that she would ever use her new-found dancing ability on a formal social occasion, but this did not destroy her pleasure in having it.

As Thomas was leaving the schoolroom, a footman arrived with the request that Lady Ashbury would like to see Mademoiselle as soon as the lessons were over. Soon after that Leonie dismissed the girls and started down the stairs to the ground floor. Passing through the marble-floored entrance hall, she paused to step into the drawing room, lingering there a few moments as she loved to do, to savour the sheer beauty of the room, with its lovely proportions, its Adam molded ceilings with the small-scale paintings by Angelica Kauffmann, its delicate furniture inlaid with gilt or marquetry and the specially woven carpet that repeated the design of the ceiling. She knew, without looking closely, that the carpet and the damask wall covering were shabby and threadbare, and she had often heard Lydia bewailing the lack of ready cash in the family budget. Mama, said Lydia, would so love to refurbish the house in the new classic style, with hieroglyphic paper on the walls, perhaps, and an ibis border to match or a monopodial table with a lion's foot. Leonie, remembering the dreadful crocodile sofa in the house of the Comte de Morville, always shuddered at the thought of this lovely old house being redecorated in the excesses of the current "Egyptian" or 'Greek" mode.

As Leonie turned to leave the drawing room, she encountered the housekeeper, Mrs. Pickering. "Could I have a moment of your time, mademoiselle?"

"Certainly, Mrs. Pickering."

"It's the butcher's account, do you see. It's quite incorrect this month. I thought perhaps that you could write to Mr. Anson to set him straight."

"I see. Well, Mrs. Pickering, I'll be very glad to bring this to Lady Ashbury's attention. I'm just going in to see her."

"Oh, very well, but you know that her ladyship will just ask you to take care of it."

Leonie smiled. "I'll be happy to do anything that Lady Ashbury asks me to do, of course. I'm sure that she'll appreciate very much your vigilance in catching Mr. Anson's mistake."

Walking on, Leonie breathed a sigh of thanks—not for the first time—that she had been able to make a niche for herself in the household without antagonising the other servants. This despite the fact that she had gradually become Lady Ashbury's strong right arm, dating from the time, soon after her arrival at Granby Court, when she had come upon Caroline in a state of near tears over a dispute that had broken out between the housekeeper and the children's old nurse, still a power in the family. Leonie had quietly and tactfully suggested a compromise that, surprisingly, both parties accepted, and from that beginning Lady Ashbury had come to seek Leonie's advice on many household and family matters.

As Leonie entered the morning room, Lady Ashbury looked up from her position on the sofa and greeted her affectionately. Except for the tired lines on her face and the fact that her blue eyes lacked the sparkle of her daughter's she could have been Lydia's older sister.

"Mrs. Pickering has asked me to consult you about the butcher's bill," began Leonie, but Lady Ashbury waved the subject away. "I know you'll deal with it beautifully, my dear. We have much more important matters to talk about. I've just had a letter from my brother Jeremy. He'll be arriving just before Christmas to spend some time with us."

"Yes, Thomas just came up to give his sisters the news. They were quite excited."

Caroline smiled. "The children are all of them so fond of Jeremy. And with good reason. One can always count on Jeremy." She sighed. "I really don't know how I could have managed last year when John got into that dreadful gambling scrape if Jeremy hadn't come to the rescue."

Leonie remained silent. Caroline was very nearly as prone as Lydia to gossip about family affairs. To change the subject, she said quickly, "Thomas spoke about giving a dance."

"Yes, I think we should do something. We've done very little entertaining for the past several years—I'm sure you've gathered that my financial circumstances have been straitened—but now that I see some light at the end of the tunnel, I would like to give a Christmas ball. Perhaps you'll help me make out the guest list—not for a grand affair, of course, just our immediate neighbors, including—" her face darkened—"the Cartwrights. Yes, I fancy we'll be obliged to invite the Cartwrights, we've known them for ages, but. . ."

Intervening hastily, to fend off any further disclosures about

Jeremy Deveril's old romance with Lady Selena, Leonie said, "I'll be very happy to help in any way that I can."

"I knew I could depend on you, dear child. Now, then, there was something else I wanted to discuss with you—oh, yes, we really must start thinking about Lydia's wardrobe for her come-out. Perhaps early next month you could go with her to Grantham—what a pity it's so far to Lincoln, or even to Boston—but we have always found Mme. Laurent to be an excellent seamstress..."

"But Lady Ashbury, might it not be better if *you* were to accompany Lydia? I've lived most of my life in a very small village, you know, and I'm certainly no expert on fashion."

"That doesn't matter at all, my dear. You have excellent taste and a good eye for colour, which poor Lydia, for all her good looks—and I *do* think she's very pretty, don't you? Not just a mother's partiality?—well, as I was saying, Lydia really does not know what suits her. Only last spring I had quite a struggle, talking her out of a bright pink lutestring that simply overpowered her colouring. And I own that I don't relish the prospect of arguing with her through an entire wardrobe for a London season. You will do much better—you know just how to manage her."

As Leonie left the morning room she recalled with a wry smile how apprehensive she had been in entering Lady Ashbury's household. At this rate, like it or not, she might soon be managing the entire establishment!

7

"MADEMOISELLE, HERE'S SOMETHING called Balm of Mecca that's supposed to do miracles for the complexion," said Lydia, from the depths of *Ackermann's Repository of the Arts, Literature, Commerce, Manufactures, Fashions and Politics*. "But it does seem very dear at four guineas the ounce, doesn't it?"

Leonie looked up from her task of preparing next day's lessons. 'At that price, it *should* perform miracles," she said tartly. "And besides, with your lovely skin, you don't need any complexion aids."

Looking not entirely convinced, Lydia returned to her fashion magazine. Classes were over for the day and she and Leonie were the only occupants of the schoolroom. Turning a page, Lydia said suddenly, "I must say, I like *this* dress much better than the one Mme. Lauent is making for me."

"Let me see." Lydia brought the magazine over to the desk and Leonie looked carefully at the coloured sketch, which depicted a morning dress in Berlin silk with wide stripes of white and lavender, topped by a jubilee cloak in purple sarcenet trimmed with swansdown. She saw at a glance that the dress was entirely wrong for Lydia, but, knowing her charge's stubborn ways, merely said, "The colour's not quite right for you. I think that the figured French cambric we agreed upon will be much more suitable."

Her forehead wrinkling mutinously, Lydia was about to give combat when Jeremy Deveril entered the room, saying, "I hope that I'm not interrupting the lessons." With a shriek of joy, Lydia jumped up to throw her arms around him.

"I'm happy that you're glad to see me, Puss," said Deveril in mock complaint as he extricated himself from Lydia's grasp, "but you're ruining the cravat that it took me half an hour to tie this morning." He was looking exceptionally well turned out, as usual, in a coat of blue superfine, molded to his powerful shoulders like a second skin, perfectly fitting buckskin breeches and shining top-boots. Leonie wondered if the coat was by Stutz or Weston, the two preeminent tailors whom young Thomas was burning to patronize when he finally made his entry on the London scene.

"Sorry, Uncle Jeremy, but it really is so wonderful to see you. We didn't expect you until much later, just before Christmas."

"Oh, well, as to that, I decided to come a bit early. London is a little thin of company at the moment. Good afternoon, mademoiselle. Have all your pupils—except for this minx, Lydia—deserted you?"

"Good afternoon, Mr. Deveril," smiled Leonie. "No, indeed, classes are over for the day. Lydia and I were just discussing her wardrobe for her London season."

"A very important subject, indubitably. What have you there, Lydia—oh, I see, *Ackermann's, La Belle Assemblée*, the *Lady's Magazine*. That should keep the pair of you busy enough."

Lydia held up the sketch of the lavender-striped morning dress. 'Uncle Jeremy,'' she said, with a sidelong look at Leonie, "don't you agree that I would look very becoming in this dress?"

Deveril flicked a glance at the fashion plate. "Certainly," he replied crushingly, "provided you were forty years of age and were trying to conceal it, *and* if you wished to drown out that lovely apple blossom colouring of yours."

"Oh," said Lydia blankly, torn between flattery and pique, and Deveril's eyes met Leonie's in a limpid look that made it clear that he had divined the clash of opinion between her and his niece.

"I'll leave you ladies to get on with your wardrobe discussion," said Deveril. "I'll see you at dinner, Lydia."

After his departure Lydia chattered on in her usual fashion. "I daresay Uncle Jeremy came early because he had word that Selena Cartwright—I mean Lady Chudleigh—was already here. Henrietta told me that her sister arrived day before yesterday."

"I've cautioned you before about gossiping," said Leonie, almost sharply, and Lydia looked up, mildly surprised.

"Oh, very well. I wasn't aware that I was *gossiping*, really... Oh, it will be so much fun having Uncle Jeremy here. Even Mama seems to enjoy life more—she doesn't seem so tired, or worry so much about John, or Thomas." She paused to look consideringly at the fashion plate. "Do you know, I think perhaps that Uncle Jeremy was right. The lavender dress really doesn't suit me."

In the days that followed Leonie came to believe that, though the old Earl of Winchcombe, with his great financial leverage, was the *éminence grise*—the ultimate power behind the scene—of the Marlowe family, it was Jeremy Deveril who effectively guided their day-to-day activities. Lady Ashbury consulted him constantly, soliciting his advice on how early to open the town house for the season or how to deal with a bad school report on William. When John, the eldest boy, came down from Cambridge for Christmas, he spent much of his time discussing John's soon-to-be-assumed duties of managing the estate. The girls, of course, quite openly adored Deveril, and Leonie soon began to feel a faint resentment at their oft-repeated dictum that "Uncle Jeremy will tell us how to do it." Thomas, anxiously waiting out the arrival of his army commission and bent on absorbing as much of his Corinthian uncle's polish and savoir faire as possible, would have monopolised most of Deveril's time had not the latter dexterously untangled himself from his nephew without, at the same time, wounding his tender sensibilities. Leonie noted with amusement that, within a few days of Deveril's arrival at Granby Court, Thomas had toned down his flamboyant apparel so that it more resembled Deveril's quiet perfection of dress. Leonie was somewhat shocked on one occasion, however, to learn from a jubilant Thomas that he had persuaded his uncle to box several rounds with him; it was her first intimation that pugilism, which her discriminating father would have considered a rather vulgar spectator sport, had become "all the crack," as Thomas put it, among the fashionable young bloods of London society. The noblest names in England flocked to take boxing lessons from Angelo, or Gentleman Jackson, the ex-champion of England, who, said Thomas, was reputed to have one-third of the peerage as his clients.

Despite his close attention to family affairs, however, Leonie did not see very much of Deveril on this Christmas visit. He was constantly out of the house, sometimes with Caroline, attending dinner parties and card parties, paying morning calls, participating in hunt meetings with the local pack. And she knew—though she tried conscientiously to cut off the flow of gossip by Lydia and her sisters—that Deveril frequently rode over to the neighbouring estate to see Lady Selena. Consequently Leonie was a little surprised, one day shortly before Christmas when she chanced to be in the library, to find Deveril smiling up at her as she stood on the ladder reaching for a book.

"Here, let me give you a hand," he said, helping her down from the ladder. "What have we here—a book on Renaissance history? Surely you're not going to assign this to Amabel and Charlotte and Augusta," he said in mock horror. "You must have gathered by this time that my nieces are not bluestockings like yourself."

Leonie felt a quite illogical—or so she told herself—little stab of disappointment. What did it matter if Deveril considered her to be a bluestocking? She had been hired as a governess, after all, and she would far rather be a bluestocking than a peagoose! "Oh, no," she said lightly, "I have no intention of forcing a book like this on the girls. I'm looking forward to reading it myself." She looked around the room. "Your late brother-in-law had a very fine collection of books."

Deveril nodded. "Yes, his grandfather imported a scholar to stock the library in his newly built 'classical' house. But I'll tell you a secret—I seriously doubt that anyone has touched one of these books since they were placed upon the shelves!"

"Surely you're exaggerating," protested Leonie with a smile.

"Perhaps just a little. I've actually read one or two myself," Deveril said, grinning. He became more serious as he added, "I've been wanting to congratulate you for the excellent work you're doing here. My sister tells me that you've been able to accomplish what poor Miss Goode was never able to do: force my nieces to sit in front of a book for more than five minutes at one time and actually learn something in the process. I also gather, from talking to Lady Ashbury, that you've taken off her hands most of her vexatious domestic problems.''

Leonie disclaimed the compliment. "Lady Ashbury is too generous. I've been able to give her a very little assistance, when she was busy with other matters."

Stepping close to her, Deveril extended his hand to brush her cheek lightly with his finger. "Don't hide your light under a bushel," he laughed, cupping her chin in his hand. "Caroline tells me that you're a treasure and that she would be hard put to do without you. As would we all!"

After Deveril had left the room, Leonie put her hand to her cheek, her thoughts seriously troubled. She knew that she was very inexperienced in the ways of society, but she was still perfectly aware that Deveril's conduct toward her had breached the bounds of propriety pertaining to the relationship between a governess and her employer's brother. His gesture of brushing her cheek might have been a mere impulse, in which case she probably need not fear any further familiarity. But if Deveril had anything more intimate in mind, Leonie realised, her days at Granby Court were likely to be numbered. She could not see herself complaining about Deveril's advances to Lady Ashbury, who in any case was far more likely to rid herself of a troublesome governess than to become embroiled with her brother. And if she did not inform Caroline about the problem, Leonie's position in the house would be insupportable, as she attempted to carry out her duties while fending off the amorous advances of Jeremy Deveril.

Leonie's feeling were so agitated during the next few days that she found herself paying very little attention to what was going on around her, until she realised in a calmer moment that Deveril, on the few occasions that she met him, had reverted to his usual polished, rather aloof self. Thus she felt no apprehension when, shortly before the day of the Christmas ball, Lydia and Thomas prevailed on Jeremy to practice their dance steps with them in the drawing room while Leonie played for them on the pianoforte. She was caught up in the rollicking gaiety of the occasion as she watched Deveril put his nieces and nephew through the paces of the country dance. She giggled along with the girls as Deveril tried to initiate the still awkward Thomas into the complicated figures of "All the Flowers of the Broom," or "Selinger's Round." "Go around twice and back again, Thomas, then set, turn and repeat. Thomas, you're not paying attention. I fear you were born with two left feet, my boy!"

As Thomas was protesting resentfully that he only needed a bit more practice, Lydia interrupted him to ask, "Do you waltz, Uncle Jeremy? Fanny writes that waltzing is much talked about, though not danced at Almack's without permission, or at Court."

"As a matter of fact, I do know at least the rudiments of the dance. A friend of mine was with her husband at the Austrian Court last year and came back entranced with the waltz. She showed us the steps in her drawing room one evening not long ago after a dinner party."

"Oh, Uncle Jeremy, please show us the steps," begged Lydia, joined by a chorus of eager seconds from Charlotte, Augusta and Amabel.

Deveril drew himself up in a mock shudder. "Indeed, I will not. I won't be held responsible for corrupting the morals of a young female who is not yet out."

"Now you're bamming us, Uncle Jeremy."

"No, I assure you, I was told by a clergyman who had seen the waltz performed in Germany that he considered it downright indecent," said Deveril, his eyes dancing. "But I'll admit to having a slightly more liberal idea on the subject." He paused, seemingly struck by a sudden idea. He snapped his fingers, saying, "Lydia, *you* play a waltz and perhaps Mademoiselle will allow me to show her the steps."

"But if the waltz isn't decent for us, Uncle Jeremy, why is it proper for Mademoiselle?" piped up Amabel.

"I'll remind you, Puss, that Mademoiselle is older than the rest of you. And then, since the waltz is danced in France, if she were living in her native country she *would* be dancing it, would she not? So in a way I consider it my civic duty to instruct her," grinned Deveril with perfect illogic. "Mademoiselle, will you oblige me?"

Leonie tried to make herself even smaller behind the pianoforte. "I would rather not. I fear that Lady Ashbury wouldn't approve."

Strolling over to the pianoforte, Deveril reached out his hand. "Nonsense. My sister will only admire your enterprise in keeping up with the current scene."

As Deveril put his arm lightly around her waist, Leonie was so flustered at the completely new sensation of being close to a man that she could not concentrate on what he was saying. She stumbled awkwardly during the first few bars of the music. Soon, however, guided by the light but insistent pressure of Deveril's hand at her waist, she was swept along in so light and airy a motion that she had the illusion of floating. All too soon the waltz came to an end, and as Deveril released her and bowed gravely, she sank into a graceful curtsey in reply.

Immediately Deveril was beset by his four nieces, all insistently clamouring for their turn. He fended them off, saying, "It's no use trying to turn me up sweet, my dears. I'll teach you how to dance the waltz when you may dance it at Almack's, and not a second before."

That evening, as Leonie sat eating her solitary dinner from a tray in her bedchamber, she found that she had little appetite. Her fears that Jeremy Deveril was making a definite bid to engage her interest, which had receded somewhat in the past day or two, were greatly heightened by his behaviour this afternoon during the dancing session in the drawing room. If he actually were to make a direct proposition to her, she reflected, she would have no choice but to resign, and she hated the very idea of leaving a secure position and this lively family that she had grown so much to like. And there was something else, a vagrant memory that she kept thrusting firmly back into the recesses of her mind, the memory of those few tremulous, gossamer moments when she had floated about the floor in the circle of Jeremy Deveril's arm.

Even before she had pushed her tray aside, a footman tapped at the door to give her Lady Ashbury's request that she come down to the drawing room to play the pianoforte for Lydia's singing. She went down, hoping that Lady Ashbury would be an audience of one, and then, as she saw Deveril sitting beside his sister, she crossed to the pianoforte without meeting his eye.

"That was lovely, Puss," said Deveril when Lydia had completed her song, and the praise was well deserved, for she had a sweet, if small, voice and had practiced conscientiously with Leonie. But of course, Leonie thought, Lydia was such a beguilingly pretty girl that even an occasional wrong note would not have spoiled her listeners' pleasure.

Blushing modestly at the compliment, Lydia said impulsively, "I thank you, Uncle Jeremy, but Mademoiselle sings far better than I do. That pretty little French ballad that you were teaching me last week, mademoiselle—you must sing it for us tonight."

"Oh, no, I couldn't think of it," replied Leonie quickly. "Lady Ashbury and Mr. Deveril aren't interested in hearing me sing."

"On the contrary, I'm persuaded that Lydia is right and

that you must have a lovely voice. My sister and I would like very much to hear you." Deveril's smile was slightly teasing and Leonie knew that he was thinking of her performance on that evening at the Comte de Morville's house.

"Yes, do give us the pleasure," said Caroline kindly, and Leonie, biting her lip as she met Deveril's amused gaze, gave in. Nervous at first, she sang well, a sad little song throbbing with tenderness and unrequited love that had been her mother's favourite.

"My dear, that was splendid. I've never heard anything I liked better, not even at the Italian Opera House," exclaimed Lady Ashbury enthusiastically. "Don't you agree, Jeremy?"

"Certainly. Mlle. de Montbarey has an exceptional voice. But then, as we all know, she is an exceptional person," said Deveril slowly, without the slightest hint of levity in his voice, and Leonie's heart sank as Caroline, her delicate eyebrows raised, shot a sudden sharp glance at her brother. Leonie resolved silently to avoid Deveril so completely in the future that there would be no opportunity for Lady Ashbury's sensitive antennae to detect the undercurrents flowing between her brother and her governess.

In actuality, Leonie had little time to worry about Deveril for the next few days as she became swept up in preparations for the Christmas dance. There had been very little entertaining in the house in recent years, owing to the financial stringency occasioned by the death of the late marquis, and the unaccustomed responsibility of the ball, added to her normal nervous disposition, would have prostrated Lady Ashbury if she had not been able to call upon Leonie to help her decide a thousand and one problems: should one of the side dishes accompanying the two main courses be a goose pie? And the principal sweet—should it be cook's magnificent hedgehog made from cream, eggs, sugar, orange flower water and canary? How many table should be set up for cards in the morning room, and how many musicians would be required for the dancing to follow? Should Lady Ashbury wear her lavender sarcenet, and might it be permissible for Amabel, just turned sixteen, to come down for the dancing, since the occasion would be an informal ball in her own home?

"There must be a diplomat or two somewhere in your ancestry, mademoiselle," teased Deveril one day when he chanced to encounter Leonie conferring with the housekeeper in the foyer. "My sister actually thinks that she is supervising all the arrangements for this ball, but of course it's you who's doing all the work."

"You're mistaken," Leonie demurred. "I'm simply carrying out Lady Ashbury's instructions."

But Deveril shook his head, laughing, as he moved away.

"If you can't be absolutely quiet, girls, I won't let you stay here," scolded Leonie in a low voice on the night of the ball, as she knelt with Augusta and Charlotte and Amabel—who would not be going downstairs until after dinner—at the top of the stairs, peering down at the entering guests.

"There's Lady Selena," breathed Amabel excitedly.

Leonie looked down at the raven-haired beauty in a gown of rose-coloured crêpe, a jewelled comb in the classical coils of her hair, her shoulders rising from the folds of a Norwich silk shawl. Lady Selena was accompanied by a man who was presumably her husband, a much older man with greying hair and a slight paunch. Leonie thought suddenly how perfectly paired Selena would be with Jeremy Deveril, whom she had seen earlier in the evening, correct and elegant in his austerely simple black evening clothes.

It was agreed by one and all next day that the Christmas ball had been a great success. Thomas, who came up midway in the evening to deliver promised treats of sweetmeats to his younger siblings, announced that he had managed to get through the country dances without once stepping on his partners' toes. Amabel, in her very first simple white ball gown, had to be forced down the stairs after an unexpected attack of nerves, but later reported in sheer bliss that she did not sit out even one dance. Lady Ashbury preened herself on the many compliments she had received on her delicious dinner and especially on the beauty of her daughters. And Lydia, who, as everyone had prophesied, was the belle of the ball, could talk of nothing but the future London triumphs that she expected to enjoy on the heels of this first success. Both Thomas and Lydia talked, at extremely great length, in Leonie's opinion, about the minor scandal occasioned when Deveril twice led Lady Selena out on the dance floor. "Because, of course, mademoiselle, it was quite the thing to ask her to dance for the first time—an old friend like that—but twice in one evening!" said Thomas. "That was doing it rather too brown!"

"*Une grenouille vit un boeuf qui lui sembla da belle taille...*" Leonie looked up from her copy of La Fontaine. "Amabel, you aren't paying attention."

"I'm sorry, mademoiselle," sighed Amabel, "but I just can't concentrate on frogs today, not when I keep thinking that Uncle Jeremy will be leaving tomorrow."

"But it's the middle of January, and Mr. Deveril has already stayed longer than you thought he would. Your mother told me that she expected him to leave right after Christmas."

"Oh, I know," said Amabel with another sigh. "But it will be so—so flat around here without Uncle Jeremy."

"Yes, we'll have nothing to look forward to until we go to London for the season," chimed in Lydia, for all the world as though she were speaking of an arid period of years rather than a scant three months.

Gazing at the young faces in front of her, Leonie found herself agreeing that a great deal of life would disappear even from this very lively family when Jeremy Deveril returned to town. And it was odd, in one sense, that he should be such an idol to his nieces and nephews, because, though he spent a great deal of time with them, he never condescended to their level. His relationship with them was always somewhat detached, that of a sophisticated, slightly aloof adult firmly in control of a group of unruly children.

"It's twelve o'clock, mademoiselle," reminded Charlotte. "You did say that we could dismiss early today so that we could go riding with Uncle Jeremy."

"I'm glad you reminded me—I'd quite forgotten. Yes, of course, you may go now."

Thomas burst into the room, giving his usual effect of a minor whirlwind. "Come along, you sluggards. The horses are all saddled. You, too, mademoiselle."

"Oh, I think not. You know that I don't participate in your guests' activities."

"Pooh," said Lydia. "Uncle Jeremy is just family."

"I was just telling him that you needed much more practice with your riding," grinned Thomas, "and he said by all means, invite Mademoiselle to come along."

"Thank you, but I have a great many things to do," began Leonie, but the girls pulled her along ruthlessly to her bedchamber, and a short time later she was walking into the stable yard, dressed in a tolerably fitting habit left behind the year before by Fanny on the occasion of her marriage.

Deveril, standing in conversation with one of the grooms, greeted Leonie with a smile. "Good afternoon, mademoiselle. Thomas tells me that you've learned to ride since you came to Granby Court."

"Good afternoon. Yes, Lady Ashbury thought that I should learn to ride so that I could accompany the girls."

Deveril nodded knowingly. "An excellent idea. A mere groom could hardly manage the four of them now that they're all such grown-up ladies who know all there is to know about riding, eh, Stubbins?"

As the aged groom nodded his rueful agreement, Leonie said, "The children insisted that I come along with you today, Mr. Deveril. I know that you probably intended this to be a family excursion."

"Not at all. I'm delighted to have your company." Deveril's words and tone were perfectly polite, but they were accompanied by the intent, disturbing look that Leonie had grown accustomed to receiving of late whenever she encountered him. She had made every effort to avoid him during the past few weeks; when they did meet he was always friendly and correct, but Leonie had the impression that there was something unsaid and under the surface between them, an invisible connection that left her painfully aware of his physical presence. She had wondered often at the change in his attitude toward her—when they had first met he had been the impersonal Lord of the Manor bestowing his bounty on a deserving underling. Perhaps his many years of coping with the problems of the Marlowe family had made it second nature for him to attempt to manage the affairs of even complete strangers with whom he came in contact. But yet, along with this earlier impersonality, there had been no suggestion of disrespect; he had seemed to treat her as a person who, though now occupying a subordinate position in society through no fault of her own, had come from roughly the same aristocratic background as his own. And there, possibly, was the key to Deveril's conduct, thought Leonie suddenly, as he held his cupped hand steady to allow her to mount the gentle hack upon which she had learned to ride. After he rescued her from the Morville house, he had learned for the first time of her clouded parentage. He would draw the line at attempting to seduce a young woman with a centuries-old ancestry; a nameless nobody might be fair game.

Her analysis of Deveril's behaviour so depressed Leonie that for some time she was oblivious to the animated chatter of the Marlowe children—all eight of them in residence had come along, including Edward and William, not yet returned to Harrow, and six-year-old George—and, as their hoof beats rang out on the lightly frozen road surface, she even failed to appreciate the delights of the crisp, clear, cold January day. But gradually, as the younger children spurred ahead, she became increasingly interested in the dialogue between Deveril and Lydia and Thomas, as his niece and nephew plied him with eager questions about London society. Lydia and Thomas listened enthralled as Deveril spun his stories about the "Ton": Beau Brummell, the "King of the Dandies," reputedly spent five hours every day on his toilette; Lord Alvanley, having once enjoyed a fresh apricot tart, ordered that one be placed on his side table every day for years in case he should fancy a slice; Lord Petersham, who collected snuffboxes, had a different one for every day of the year. When, however, Deveril's talk turned to such activities as the showings at the Royal Academy, or Kemble's playing of Falstaff, Lydia and Thomas, never very interested in cultural matters, drifted off to race with their siblings, and Leonie found herself riding alone with Deveril.

"You ride very well," he said politely.

"Oh, I thank you, but give all the credit to this old horse. Thomas says that the merest baby could ride him," said Leonie nervously. "Mr. Deveril, I think we really should catch up with the others." She struck her mount sharply with her riding crop, and the ordinarily placid beast, starting at the unexpected blow, had the added misfortune to encounter a rabbit streaking out of a copse at a bend of the road. The horse bounded forward and Leonie dropped from the saddle. She lost consciousness for a few moments, awakening to find her head and shoulders supported by Deveril's arm.

"Mlle. de Montbarey—Leonie—are you all right?" he asked anxiously. "Do you hurt anywhere? Your head, your arms and legs?"

Leonie stirred, pushing herself away from Deveril, and rose shakily to her feet. "No, I'm not hurt at all," she assured him, ruefully looking down at her habit, liberally streaked with road dust and bits of dried vegetation. "I think that I'm more mortified than anything else," she added. "I simply slid off that horse, like a rag doll, or a—a bundle of hay!" She raised her head, her face dimpling with self-laughter, and Deveril, who had moved solicitously closer to her, said huskily, "You're such a sobersides most of the time, but when you smile like that, you're enchanting!" Before Leonie, her eyes widening in alarm, could pull away, Deveril crushed her to him, seeking her mouth in a bruising kiss that set her heart to pounding and her blood to coursing fiercely through her veins. She was exquisitely aware of his masculine magnetism so close to her. His questing lips moved hungrily to her closed eyelids and down to her throat, and then as his mouth closed down on hers again Leonie shuddered and strained away from him, beating her hands against his shoulders, and when that proved ineffectual, grabbing a handful of his hair. He released her suddenly, stumbling back and breathing hard, while his face wore a curiously dazed expression.

"I'm sorry," he muttered. "I don't know. . ."

"How dare you—how dare you force yourself on me," exclaimed Leonie, her voice shrill with outrage, an outrage even more vehement, perhaps, because she knew, deep within her heart, that there had been at least a moment when she had been tempted to yield to the violence of Deveril's emotions.

The dazed expression disappeared, and Deveril, flushing a deep red, said stiffly, "I fully understand your anger, but I assure you, I had no intention of taking advantage of you, of 'forcing' myself on you. What I did was simply a spontaneous reaction—I was so concerned that you had hurt yourself in your fall, and then—you looked so lovely. . ."

"Is that the excuse that you offer to every scullery wench or chambermaid that you meet?" flashed Leonie.

Deveril's embarrassed crimson faded, and he said, in tones of rapidly mounting anger, "Are you now accusing me of attempting to seduce every woman who crosses my path?"

"Not at all," replied Leonie recklessly, her own anger growing red-hot to the point of irrationality. "I'm sure that you restrict yourself to females well beneath you on the social scale. Shopgirls and maidservants and governesses. Or am I doing you an injustice, Mr. Deveril? Am I, perhaps, the first governess who has caught your eye?"

Pale now with barely controlled rage, his hand clenched so tightly that the knuckles showed white through the skin, Deveril stepped back with a bow. "I thank you for making your opinion of my character so abundantly clear," he said levelly. "There being little left for us to say, I suggest that we rejoin your charges."

"As you wish." In complete silence, Deveril caught the reins of Leonie's hack, which had remained, quietly cropping grass, in the immediate vicinity and brought the horse over to her. Still without speaking, he held his hand to assist her to mount, and, as she cantered away, touched his hat politely.

Struggling against her seething emotions, Leonie arrived back at Granby Court in so agitated a state that old Stubbins, the groom, who came running up to catch her bridle, asked anxiously, "Are you ill, Miss? You look terrible pale."

"No, thank you, Stubbins, I'm quite all right."

Leonie escaped to her bedchamber without encountering a

servant or any member of the family and threw herself on her bed. Feverishly she went over in her mind every detail of her unsettling encounter with Jeremy Deveril. In the end, though her feelings were still deeply lacerated by the denigrating arrogance of his overtures, she was beginning to wish that her own response had been more dignified. If there had ever been a chance that she might retain her position here at Granby Court after this incident, that chance was probably now gone: no matter, even, if Deveril came to regret his behaviour to her, he would never be able to bring himself to overlook the wounding accusations she had thrown at him. As Leonie listened to the faint sounds from the stable yard, signalling the return of the riding party, she lay stiffly on her bed, expecting at any moment to receive a summons to speak to Lady Ashbury about her dismissal.

8

"LOOK, WILL, TWO kinds of bears! And there's a lion in that other cage over there," said Edward enthusiastically, and Leonie gave a little sigh of relief as she realised that the sightseeing trip to the Tower of London was going to be much more popular with the Marlowe children than the other expeditions for which she had been their guide and mentor during the past few weeks. They loved the Tower Zoo best of all, of course, but they had also enjoyed the Armoury, with the sword that had beheaded Anne Boleyn, and their eyes had widened at the sight of the crown jewels, guarded in their dark vault by a toothless old hag.

On previous afternoons, the young Marlowes, as little inclined toward cultural matters as Thomas and Lydia, had been quite bored with the House of Commons, though even they looked askance at members who were eating oranges or cracking nuts or lying full length on the benches while other members were making speeches; they were completely uninterested in the British Museum; and they were in a state of outright rebellion at the Royal Academy, refusing even to look at the lovely Constable paintings of their own flat East Anglian countryside.

In her idle moments, Leonie often pondered on the contrast between her present busy, satisfying life in London and that other period last year when she had been jobless and unfamiliar with this vast city, and, after her experience with the Comte de Morville, frightened and apprehensive about her future. She had not seen Deveril since their tumultuous set-to at Granby Court early in the new year, and, after it became apparent that he was not going to mention the encounter to his sister, she had thankfully succeeded in putting him very thoroughly out of her mind. Her days were both full and secure as she continued to teach the younger girls, act as Lady Ashbury's unofficial housekeeper and supervise Lydia's coming out.

Of Lydia personally, once that young lady was dressed for the day, or the evening, Leonie actually saw very little. Lydia's life was an exhausting round of balls and routs and assemblies, ton parties, breakfasts and theatre parties, on which she appeared to thrive with boundless energy. With the arrival of Edward and William from Harrow began the series of instructive sightseeing trips, which Leonie heartily enjoyed even if her charges did not. Thomas she saw infrequently, even though he was in London with the family, waiting out his commission, revelling in his visits to the fashionable haunts he had long been dreaming of: Angelo's Academy for boxing lessons, the Daffy Club for professional fights, Hoby's for boots and Weston's to be measured for a suit, and Tattersall's near Hyde Park Corner for a wistful, though no-buying, look at prime horseflesh. Leonie's thoughts lingered on Thomas; for the past several days he had stayed at home much more than usual, and he had seemed only the shadow of his usual ebullient self. Something was obviously bothering Thomas, and Leonie determined that she would have a tactfully probing talk with him.

As soon as she was able to tear them away from the delights of the Tower Zoo, Leonie herded the children into the carriage and gave the order to return to Cavendish Square. Rounding the circular railed enclosure in the middle of the square, the carriage pulled up before a gracious pillared house on the north side. Ashbury House had been shuttered and vacant most of the time since the death of the late marquis and the discovery of the shaky family financial position, but it had been opened for Fanny's debut the year before, and now again for Lydia's season. As Leonie and the children piled out of the carriage, she noticed an elegant town carriage drawn up before the door, a waiting coachman on the box. When the party entered the house, the butler drew Leonie aside to tell her that Lady Ashbury would like to see her in the drawing room.

"Thank you, Chesley. I will join Lady Asbury as soon as I've taken off my bonnet." Mounting the stairs, Leonie idly wondered why she had been summoned to see Lady Ashbury when the latter already had a visitor, judging by the evidence of the chariot at the door. In her bedroom, Leonie quickly ran a comb through her hair and placed upon it the muslin cap which she habitually wore indoors because it hid the bright hair that in her opinion made her look so unlike a governess. She smoothed down her plain grey muslin dress, and, after one last look in the mirror, stepped out into the corridor where she nearly collided with Thomas, just emerging from his bedchamber.

"Hello there, mademoiselle," he greeted her. "Have you been admitted to the Presence?"

"Whatever do you mean, Thomas?"

"Haven't you heard? Our uncle is downstairs visiting

Mama, and I heard him tell her that he wanted to meet the new governess."

"No, I hadn't heard about it," said Leonie slowly, with a slightly hollow feeling in the pit of her stomach at the thought of meeting the redoubtable patriarch of the family. Then she looked at Thomas more closely. His sprightly tone had seemed forced and his expression distinctly subdued. She said quietly, "Thomas, are you blue-devilled about something?"

"Certainly not," said Thomas promptly. "Whatever gave you such an idea? Matter of fact, you're being the outside of enough, since my uncle has just given me the news that my commission has come through. I'm to serve under General Sir Thomas Picton in the 74th."

"Thomas! I'm so happy for you!" exclaimed Leonie delightedly. She paused, an anxious frown furrowing her forehead. "I suppose that means that you'll be with General Wellesley in the Peninsula?"

"He's Lord Wellington now," Thomas corrected her. "And yes, I will be going to the Peninsula." For a young man who had been awaiting the arrival of his commission so anxiously and for so long, Thomas seemed curiously disinclined to talk about his triumph. Instead, he excused himself on the grounds of a prior urgent engagement.

"I suppose you're off to take another boxing lesson," joked Leonie.

Momentarily a gleam of his usual lightheartedness returned to Thomas's expression. "Now, don't you be so top-lofty," he grinned. "Not all my amusements are as low-minded as you seem to think. *This* time I'm going to see a cricket match in Dorset Square."

Her thoughts preoccupied with Thomas's possible plight as she walked down the stairs, Leonie was quite mentally unprepared for her first glimpse of his uncle. The Earl of Winchcombe was an impressive, if not actually intimidating figure. Well over six feet tall, powerfully built, he wore breeches and topboots instead of the more fashionable pantaloons, and his thick hair was worn powdered in a queue, a hair style seldom seen these days since the imposition of the wartime tax on hair powder in 1795. The earl had very thick white eyebrows and piercing, chilly blue eyes that fixed on Leonie unnervingly as she made her curtsey.

"Sit down, mademoiselle," he barked, in a tone that conveyed an aura of unquestioned authority. "My nieces have been telling me a great deal about you."

Leonie bowed her head slightly, stealing a glance at Lady Ashbury seated on a sofa beside an uncharacteristically quiet Lydia.

"They tell me that you're a very accomplished young woman," continued the earl. "I should have thought an older woman—and English at that—would have been preferable, but that's neither here nor there, I suppose. Now then: your father instructed you in history and literature?" The earl proceeded to pick his way ruthlessly through Leonie's educational background, revealing in passing that he himself was a very cultivated man. He tried out her Italian—his own accent was surprisingly good—and ended by rigorously quizzing her knowledge of music. After the interrogation, Leonie felt as if she had been dipped into a tub of water, twisted to remove the excess moisture and hung out to dry. But the earl, with no change of expression on his coldly impassive face, merely gave a curt nod and turned his attention to Lydia.

"Well, my dear—" he searched his mind—"Lydia, is it? My dear Lydia, I presume that you're having an enjoyable and successful first season?"

"Oh, yes, Uncle," Lydia assured him in a small voice.

"Racketing about every morning and all day long too, I suppose," commented the earl. "Oh, well, I daresay that's how things are done these days. Mind, I don't want to hear anything about your falling to the charms of the first caper-witted handsome Guards officer who comes your way. Your portion will be very small, and you must think of your mother and your brothers and sisters."

"Oh, no, Uncle," breathed Lydia, her pretty, vivacious little face flushing a bright red.

"Now, my dear, no need to turn girlish on me," said the earl indulgently. "I'm sure that you'll act just as you ought." Turning to Caroline, he asked, "Have you decided on the details of Lydia's coming-out party?"

"There's not a great deal to decide, Uncle. We thought it best to plan on giving just a dinner party."

"Not a ball?" asked the earl in surprise. Then his brow cleared in understanding, and he added, "You're thinking of the expense, I presume. Now, my dear Caroline, I beg you not to be so foolish. I've told you time and again that I would assume all the charges. Lydia's party must be in the first style of elegance."

"But Uncle, you've already done so much for us..."

"Nonsense. I pray you, don't talk such fustian." The earl swung his gaze to Lydia. "I'll wager that you have some very definite ideas of your own, young lady."

"Well," began Lydia hesitatingly, "I did mention a costume ball to Mama, but she said no."

After a moment or two of judicious thought, the earl said, "I see nothing wrong with the idea. Mind you, I won't countenance a masked ball, which has always smacked to me of the demimonde. But a costume ball, why, certainly."

During the remaining portion of the earl's visit, Leonie studied him carefully, thinking with amusement that one could easily believe that he was Jeremy Deveril's grandfather, rather than the distant cousin he actually was. There was a certain physical resemblance—both were tall, powerful men, with well-shaped heads and strong, handsome features—

but even more pronounced was the identical air of calm authority, of unthinking arrogance, that characterised them. In their attitude toward Caroline and her family, however, Leonie thought that she could discern a difference: the earl's chilly manner suggested not so much a personal interest in the Marlowe family as a rigid sense of duty toward them; whereas in Jeremy Deveril, detached though he so often appeared to be with the children, withholding a portion of himself, she had never doubted his real affection for them.

When the earl had taken his leave, bowing to each of the women with his careful, old-fashioned formality, Lydia jumped up and skipped about the room in ecstasy. "Oh, Mama," she exclaimed, "It will be such heaven, holding a costume ball. It will be the talk of the town. All my friends will be green with envy. What shall I wear? Mademoiselle, I daresay you can think of a dozen ideas for a costume. I wonder how I would look as a Greek statue come to life—Persephone, perhaps with a wreath of flowers in my hair..."

"If that's the statue that I'm thinking about, you can forget about it," declared Caroline, with what was for her unusual asperity. "You'll go to your ball fully clothed, Lydia, if I have to find you a nun's habit! Run along upstairs, child; I want you to get a little rest before you go out to Almack's this evening."

After Lydia's departure, Caroline motioned for Leonie to come sit beside her on the sofa. "I'm so happy that my uncle was so impressed with you.

"Frankly, I thought that he seemed something less than enthusiastic."

"Oh, no, my dear, you quite mistake him. He definitely approved of you. One is never in any doubt whatsoever about Uncle's approval." Lady Ashbury sighed. "I daresay some would judge me very poor-spirited in my attitude toward my uncle, but I feel bound to bow to his opinions in almost everything—he has been excessively generous to me and my older children already, and there are all the others to be established. Even Jeremy, so forceful and independent, would think twice before crossing him, I'll be bound. Just today Uncle came to tell us that Thomas's commission has finally come through, and he also mentioned again that a living would be available for Edward or William whenever they were in a position to accept it.''

At Lady Ashbury's last statement, Leonie broke into an involuntary gurgle of laughter, and, after a startled moment, Caroline joined in. "I know what you're thinking—neither Edward nor William is cut out to be a clergyman—though I often think that an enforced retreat as tonsured monks would do both of them a world of good!"

"We'll finish much more quickly if you hold your head still," said Leonie that evening as she stood behind Lydia putting the final touches to the girl's feathery dark curls. Leonie's fingers were so much more deft than her own that Lydia's maid had relinquished her hairdressing duties without a shade of resentment.

Her hair arranged, Lydia, looking exquisitely lovely in her gown of sheerest white muslin, pirouetted expectantly before the cheval glass. Two months of attendance had not palled her enthusiasm for Almack's Assembly Rooms, where a ball and a supper were given once a week during the twelve week "season." Almack's was controlled by a powerful board of patronesses from the highest ranks of society, each of whom was allowed a limited number of vouchers. It was said that, of the three hundred Guards' officers resident in London at any one time, only six were granted vouchers for Almack's. It spoke volumes for the security of Lydia's social position, Leonie often thought, that there had never been the shadow of a doubt that she would be among the lucky few to obtain a voucher.

A tap sounded at the door and Leonie opened it to find Thomas standing in the corridor, very smart in his black coat with gilt buttons, tight kerseymere knee breeches and buckled shoes, his chapeau bras tucked under his arm. "Tell Lydia that she's preened herself long enough. It's time to go."

"She'll be out in a moment. You're looking very handsome tonight, Thomas. You'll cut a swath through all the girlish hearts tonight."

"Nothing of the sort, mademoiselle. You know that I still have two left feet. And I must say, going to Almack's is getting to be a dead bore. All those insipid girls and their Gorgon mothers, and the refreshments!—just lemonade and tea and bread and butter and stale cake."

These glum remarks were so at odds with Thomas's normally buoyant nature that Leonie, moved by impulse, said, "I'd like to talk to you, just for a moment or two." She reached back into Lydia's room for a candle and motioned Thomas ahead of her into the empty schoolroom.

"Now, then," she confronted him after she had closed the door, "I want you to tell me what's troubling you—no, don't deny it. Anyone with half an eye can see that you're fretting about something."

"I don't—" began Thomas stiffly. Then, as he met Leonie's steady gaze, he lowered his head, mumbling, "Well, yes, perhaps I do have a problem of sorts, but nothing that need concern you. I can perfectly well deal with it myself."

"Oh, indeed? It's been over a week now since I first suspected that you were in some kind of predicament, and, if your hag-ridden looks are any indication, you haven't made any progress toward a solution. Really, Thomas, it might help just to talk about it."

"Dash it, not the sort of thing you can discuss with a lady," said Thomas obstinately.

"But I'm not a lady. I'm just a governess." As Thomas's face broke into a reluctant grin, Leonie pressed on. "I'm quite sure that you're no loose fish"—Thomas's eyes widened—"isn't that your slang for libertine? So I suspect that you've been gambling and that you've lost much more money than is good for you. Am I right?"

Thomas's young face crumpled. "I'm deep in dun territory," he said despairingly. "Mademoiselle, I owe five hundred pounds! It's not a huge sum, I suppose, but I haven't a farthing of my own, and I just can't ask Mama for it, not after all the troubles she had last year with my brother John."

"Not a huge sum!" exclaimed Leonie, horrified. "It's a small fortune. I can see that you don't like to ask your mother for it, but how about your uncle Jeremy?"

"I can't ask him for the money. Not after he put me up for White's and Boodle's and expressly warned me against wasting my blunt like Papa and John. And I *did* remember his warning," Thomas added self-righteously. "I didn't wager a penny at the clubs. Wasn't even tempted to, when I heard those old stories about Fox losing 140,000 pounds before he was twenty-five, or Sir John Bland gambling away the whole city of Manchester. But I saw nothing wrong in placing small bets on a cockfight, or a prize fight or a horse race—and then suddenly a week or so ago I added up all those small losses and they amounted to over five hundred pounds."

"I see," said Leonie slowly. "I wish I had five hundred pounds, I'd gladly give it to you. But I do have one piece of advice that I *know* is good. Go straight to your uncle Jeremy. He might be a little angry, just at first, but I'm sure that he would help you."

"No. I can't and I won't do that. I'll think of something. There are always the money-lenders. They charge a fearful interest, but I have my commission now, I could pay back the loan a little at a time."

The next afternoon, as she accompanied Augusta, Amabel and Charlotte on the brisk daily stroll that was a real necessity for these country-bred girls, cooped up all day in their city residence, Leonie's thoughts were focussed on Thomas; even her scanty experience in society had given her some indication of the perils of falling into the clutches of the moneylenders, and she was very concerned that the boy might do something that would compromise his whole future.

As the walkers turned into Cavendish Square they saw Jeremy Deveril driving up before Ashbury House in a sporting phaëton with high double perches and a team of matched greys. When the girls broke ranks to run up to him, inquiring noisily where he had been for the past weeks, he greeted them with his usual detached affection, informing them that he had been at his country estate. "It doesn't manage itself, you know."

Leonie felt a perverse little pang when Deveril turned to greet her with a reserved formal courtesy, so different from the half-teasing, half-familiar tone he had fallen into using with her during the latter part of the Christmas holidays at Granby Court.

Amabel was looking enviously at Deveril's equipage. "We've heard that high-perch phaëtons were all the crack now. Yours is in the first style of elegance, Uncle. And those greys! When did you get them?"

"Yesterday, as a matter of fact. Friend of mine needed a bit of the ready, so I took his team off his hands."

"I'll wager they're sweet goers. Uncle, couldn't we have a ride? Driving in the park with Mama is so—so tame!"

As Charlotte and Augusta opened their mouths, preparing to chime in, Deveril said, "Oh, very well, I'll take you up,

Amabel, but you two will have to wait for another time." He motioned to his tiger to jump down.

"I'm sorry, Mr. Deveril," said Leonie regretfully, glancing at her watch. "I fear that none of the girls can drive with you. The seamstress is coming this afternoon to measure them for their winter wardrobes."

Amid a chorus of groans, Deveril said suddenly, "Well, if I can't have any of my nieces to keep me company, mademoiselle, supposing that I take you?"

"No, I thank you. I have a great many things to do this afternoon." The words popped out instinctively in reply to the cool, imperious manner in which the invitation had been extended, but almost immediately the image of Thomas's worried young face flashed into Leonie's mind. "On second thought, I believe it would be quite an experience to ride in a high-perch phaëton. May I change my mind?"

While the girls watched her with good-natured though still envious eyes, Deveril's groom helped Leonie into her alarmingly high seat and the phaëton moved off. She looked down nervously at the roadway far below, and Deveril said reassuringly, "Please don't be frightened. I promise you that I won't overturn you. My nieces will tell you that I'm a perfectly safe driver."

"Oh, I'm well aware that you're at home to a peg, Mr. Deveril. Recall, I've driven with you before. Of course, it's highly improper, as you know as well as I do, for you to invite the family governess for a social drive."

"And yet you came," Deveril replied promptly, with a slanting sideways look.

Leonie sighed. "Yes, I did. This one time. I wanted to talk to you about Thomas, and this seemed like a good opportunity to see you privately." As they continued on through the side streets surrounding Cavendish Square, with their formal rectangular patterns and neatly terraced brick homes, Leonie gave Deveril the details of Thomas's gambling debts. "I begged him to go to you, but he didn't feel that he could do that, after your repeated warnings about gambling."

Deveril shook his head heavily. "I've been afraid of this, frankly. The gambling streak seems to run in the Marlowe family."

"Oh, I don't think Thomas is a real gambler. I believe that he fell into the habit of placing small bets more to keep up with his fashionable young friends than for any other reason. If you will just help him out this once, I feel there's a very good chance that he has gotten it out of his system."

"I hope very much that you're right. Gambling can be a curse. I've seen it ruin whole families. And I'm sure that you're well aware of my sister's financial difficulties, caused by her husband's enormous losses at the tables."

"I'm very sure about Thomas. I'd stake my life on his soundness," said Leonie firmly. "But I have a favour to ask of you. Please don't let Thomas suspect that I came to you with his problem. He'd see it as a betrayal of his confidence."

Deveril turned his head with a look of real gratitude. "I won't," he promised. "I'll make an opportunity to speak to Thomas and ferret out his secret in such a way that he'll never realise that I knew all about it beforehand. At any rate, he won't have much further opportunity to get into mischief— not in London. He'll soon be off to his regiment."

"That will mean fighting, will it not?"

"Yes," said Deveril quietly. "Heavy fighting, I fear." He was silent for a moment, then said abruptly, "I, too, had a reason for asking you to come driving with me. I would like to apologise to you for my most ungentlemanly conduct at our last meeting at Granby Court. I did act out of pure impulse, as I tried to tell you at the time. You implied that I tried to take advantage of what I considered your inferior social position. Mademoiselle, such a thought was never in my mind."

Deveril's words certainly constituted a handsome apology, but Leonie felt curiously let down. Deveril's voice was impersonally formal. There was little evidence that the apology came from the heart; perhaps he was only offering it because he felt duty bound, because he owed it to his position.

After a long pause, Leonie said slowly, "Thank you. Perhaps I, too, owe you an apology. I was probably overly hasty in my remarks to you—you see, I thought your behaviour to me had changed, had become more familiar, after you learned that I wasn't really the daughter of the Baron de Montbarey. For all you knew, I suppose, I could have been the daughter of a peasant, or a—a person of ill repute."

Deveril's brows drew together. "You're glaringly abroad, mademoiselle," he said with finality. "I know quite well who you are. Oh, not your real name or your place of origin. But I can recognise quality when I see it."

"Oh." Leonie fell silent, totally unable to think of any thing to say. Deveril, too, was silent. There was an almost palpable feeling of constraint between them as they drove along Wigmore Street to Portman Square. There, as they made the circuit of the square, preparatory to returning to Ashbury House, Leonie idly noted a young man walking along the pavement. As the phaëton came up to him, the young man lifted his head. Startled, Leonie stared unbelievingly at Robert Linton, who, equally startled, had time only for a sketchy bow before the phaëton rattled out of Portman Square.

9

"You don't even look like the same person, Thomas. You look so—so grown-up!" exclaimed Amabel.

"You look beautiful," said Charlotte, equally lost in admiration of her elder brother. Thomas had come to the classroom—where Leonie was insisting on a brief daily session even during the holiday period—to show off his brand-new regimentals, which had been languishing in unseen splendour at the military outfitter's against the day when he could take up his commission.

Thomas turned slowly so that his sisters could get the full effect of the scarlet coat, laced in green and sashed in crimson, the white kerseymere breeches, the buff leather crossbelt with the silver plate marked with the "74" and the cocked hat of black felt topped with a plume of cut feathers. Curiously, Leonie thought, he managed at the same time to look more mature, as Amabel suggested, and heart-breakingly young.

It was obvious that Amabel, Charlotte and Augusta were

ill-prepared to concentrate after the excitement of Thomas's new regimentals, so Leonie dismissed the girls for the day. Lingering until his sisters had left the room, Thomas closed the door behind them, saying, "I've been wanting a word with you, mademoiselle. I thought that you'd be glad to learn that I've solved my problem. Uncle Jeremy is going to loan me the money to pay off my debts."

"I'm so happy for you," exclaimed Leonie. Mentally crossing her fingers, she asked innocently, "So you decided to go to Mr. Deveril after all? I was hoping that you would."

"Well, no, as a matter of fact. I chanced to meet him just yesterday at Gentleman Jackson's and we got to chatting, as people do, you know, and I suppose he could see that I was blue-devilled. Anyway, before I knew what he was about, he had guessed that I was at point-non-plus. A very wary bird, my uncle, awake on every suit. I consider the money just a loan, of course; I intend to give him practically every penny of my pay until the debt is cancelled."

Leonie suspected that more than chance was responsible for Jeremy Deveril's meeting with his nephew. She could easily imagine Deveril going from haunt to popular haunt until his final "accidental" encounter with Thomas.

"So there's no need to worry about me any more," said Thomas. "Uncle Jeremy warned me off all gambling in the future, but I had already decided never to be so hen-witted again. I'll have quite enough to do, helping Lord Wellington chase Boney's generals out of the Peninsula! Oh, by the way," he added as an afterthought as he was leaving, "Met an acquaintance of yours yesterday, too. Fellow I knew up at Cambridge—Robert Linton. Said he saw you driving with Uncle Jeremy the other day—recognised Uncle, of course, he's almost as well known as the Beau. Said you used to be governess to his sisters. Asked me to give you his regards."

"That was kind of Lord Linton," said Leonie, trying for a casualness that she did not feel. She had been hoping that her momentary glimpse of Robert Linton would be her only contact with him; it was hardly possible for a young man in his position to call upon a servant in someone else's house. "Were you—er—well acquainted with Lord Linton at Cambridge?"

"Lord, no. Scarcely recognised him, matter of fact. He was a very quiet, studious sort of fellow. Seems nice enough, though."

Leonie could easily believe in the unlikelihood of a friendship between Thomas and the shy, retiring, bookish Robert. A somewhat disquieting thought crossed her mind: Robert, though shy, was also both persistent and single-minded; he had probably sought out Thomas's company very deliberately after seeing her with Jeremy Deveril in Portman Square.

Leonie sighed, thrusting the problem of Robert into the back of her mind, as she went down the stairs to keep a promised appointment with Lady Ashbury.

Caroline was sitting at her desk in the morning room, looking more than a little worn from days and nights of chaperoning Lydia on her never-ending round of social activities. "And to think, mademoiselle," she said tragically, "that I will have it all to do over again with Amabel and Charlotte and Augusta. I vow, it almost makes one wish that all one's children had been boys!"

Suppressing a smile, Leonie said helpfully, as she seated herself near Lady Ashbury, "Perhaps Lady Fanny could take charge of one or all of them. Didn't you tell me that she would have undertaken to bring Lydia out, if only she hadn't been increasing?"

Lady Ashbury brightened. "That's so. Fanny would like nothing better than to bring out one of her sisters—Fanny adores parties. Or if Lydia marries early, in her first or second season, *she* could do so."

"That's more than likely, don't you think? Lydia is such a pretty girl, and has so many admirers."

"Thank you, my dear. I do believe that is so. Did I tell you, Lord Manville was very particular in his attention to Lydia at Lady Donnington's rout party last week? She seemed to like him very well, too. It would be an excellent match." Lady Ashbury shook herself from her pleasant reverie. "Well, now to business. I must thank you again for being so helpful to me at this very busy time. I just could not have coped with Lydia's costume ball without you." She picked up a paper from her desk. "I see that you've drawn up the entire menu. It looks perfect to me. You're sure that the ices will be in good supply at the time of the ball?"

"I believe so. I went to Gunther's because I saw their announcement in the *Times* saying that they had received a cargo of ice from the Greenland Seas and were again able to supply cream and fruit ices at their former prices."

"Excellent. And now, what about the orchestra?"

"I've contacted Mr. Felton, since you told me that Lady Castlereagh had recommended him. But he will be very expensive."

Lady Ashbury looked up with a thankful smile. "That will be all right, my dear. For once, thanks to my uncle, I need spare no expense. Engage Mr. Felton's orchestra, by all means. That leaves only Lydia's costume. Has she told you that she wants to appear as Cleopatra?"

"Yes, I think she will make an enchanting Cleopatra."

"But mademoiselle, have you thought—I've heard that

ancient Egyptian ladies sometimes were not—you know—always fully clothed."

"Don't look so alarmed," laughed Leonie. "I've seen the sketch. The dress will have a very wide jewelled collar. Lydia will be rather more fully clothed than she would be in one of her ball gowns."

Caroline's harried frown relaxed. "That's all we need settle at this time, then." Putting aside her papers, she prepared to rise, then put a hand to her forehead, saying faintly, "Oh, dear, my wretched headache has come back."

"You've been staying up very late since you came to London," said Leonie sympathetically. "You're used to more regular hours."

"I fear you're right." Caroline hesitated. "I would like so much to rest this afternoon. Dear mademoiselle, you are so good always, could I possibly ask you to chaperon Lydia in the park today?"

Leonie had, of course, walked in Hyde Park on several occasions with Lydia's younger sisters, but she had never before been there at *the* fashionable hour of 5 P.M., when every lady of any consequence in London society appeared in an open barouche with a coachman up front and a liveried, bewigged footman behind, and all the dandies and Corinthians displayed their skills behind the reins of a dashing pair attached to the latest model phaëton or curricle, or rode a showy mount from Tattersall's that had probably cost not a penny less than 1,000 guineas.

Soon after she drove into the park with Lydia in the Ashbury barouche, Leonie began to realise just how much her former pupil had matured—at least on the surface—from the coltish, rather awkward, though always beautiful, young girl who had arrived in London at the beginning of the season. Leonie could only admire the poise with which Lydia returned the constant bows from beautifully dressed ladies in their carriages, or the practised ease with which she parried the addresses of the swarm of eager young men who besieged her, on foot or on horseback, all the while pointing out to Leonie in a low voice the identity of the notables who thronged the park. Lydia introduced one handsome youngster, who could not seem to tear himself away from the Ashbury carriage, as Lord Manville; after studying the pair for a few moments, Leonie agreed with Lady Ashbury that a match was probably imminent.

"Mlle. de Montbarey? What a pleasant surprise."

Her heart sinking, Leonie looked to her right to see Robert Linton's beaming face as he and a companion came abreast of the carriage on horseback.

"A friend of yours, mademoiselle?" Lydia signalled the coachman to stop.

As Robert reined in his mount, Leonie said, as calmly as she could, "Lady Lydia Marlowe, may I present Viscount Linton?"

"I'm honored, Lady Lydia. I'm acquainted with your brother," said Robert gallantly, making an obvious effort to tear his eyes away from Leonie long enough to bow over Lydia's pretty hand. "Lady Lydia, Mlle. de Montbarey, I would like to introduce my friend, the Comte de Morville."

"The comte and I are already acquainted," said Leonie, dry-mouthed, as she stared back into Morville's hooded black eyes.

"Lady Lydia, mademoiselle, I am honoured," said the comte, bowing gracefully from the saddle. "Yes," he nodded to Robert, "Mlle. de Montbarey and I are old friends. I was not, of course, aware that she also knew you."

"Mademoiselle was governess to my sisters for several years," smiled Robert guilelessly.

"Indeed? How very interesting. I am sure that Mademoiselle was very proficient at her duties."

Cringing inwardly at the concealed mockery in the comte's silken tones, Leonie was happy to see him transfer his attentions to Lydia. Robert took advantage of the cover afforded by their animated conversation to dismount and speak confidentially to Leonie. "I can't believe my good fortune in meeting you today," he murmured happily. "I've been wracking my brains, trying to discover a way to contact you—I know Lord Thomas Marlowe, of course, but my stepmama and Lady Ashbury are not acquainted..."

"It would make no difference if Lady Linton did know my employer," snapped Leonie with considerable asperity. "You know very well, Robert, that you could not call on Lady Ashbury's governess."

Robert looked pained. "But mademoiselle, I thought that we were friends. I certainly don't think of you as just a governess. I know that you refused to let me write to you, after you left us at Wanstead Abbey, for fear of what Mama would say. But you must agree that my situation is entirely different now: I've turned eighteen years of age, and even Mama can scarcely continue to dictate to me who my friends should be."

"I think that you'll find that she has every intention of doing just that," replied Leonie drily. "Especially where I'm concerned." She countered Robert's obvious intention to dispute her statement by changing the subject. She raised her voice, saying, "And how are your mother and your sisters? Are they in town?"

"Yes. Mama has just put off her blacks. She opened the town house last week. She seems very happy to be back in London. I think perhaps that she was getting very bored toward the end of her year of mourning."

"Is Lady Linton well acquainted with the Comte de Morville?" asked Leonie, almost in spite of herself.

Overhearing her, the comte turned smilingly from Lydia.

"No, not at all. Lady Linton and I have just met. But I can tell already, it is going to be a distinct pleasure to know such a beautiful lady. England, for impressionable Frenchmen like myself, seems full of beautiful ladies," he added, bowing slightly to both Lydia and Leonie. Shortly afterwards he and Robert took their leave to continue to ride in the park, and Lydia remarked, as their carriage started off again, "What a charming man—the comte, I mean. Have you known him long, mademoiselle?"

"No, not very long," replied Leonie shortly, and began to talk about the Prince Regent, who, passing by with his equerry, had just bowed to Lydia with considerable grace despite his great obesity.

But though it was easy enough to dismiss the Comte de Morville from a conversation, Leonie found it much more difficult to dismiss him from her mind. Through the rest of the day and into the next, she experienced great feelings of foreboding; she was certain that she had not seen the last of the comte in her life. Her foreboding was justified, at least to some extent, when a servant brought her a letter the next day, a letter addressed in a spidery hand that was quite unfamiliar to her.

"My dear Mlle. de Montbarey," the letter read in French. "I was so surprised and so very pleased to learn this morning from my old friend the Comte de Morville that you were still—or perhaps back—in London. In the months since I last saw you I have thought of you often, and wondered how you were getting on. I would like so much to see you again. Could you join me for a little talk and glass of wine this coming Friday? I hope to see you at eleven o'clock. I remain, very faithfully yours, Suzanne de Vaucouleurs."

It had really been quite remiss on her part, thought Leonie guiltily, not to have contacted Mme. de Vaucouleurs, after the comtesse had received her so graciously at the house in Baker

Street. It was unlikely that she and the elderly émigré noblewoman would ever be close, but at the very least, in consideration of the comtesse's long friendship with the elder de Montbareys, Leonie should have written to tell her of her employment with Lady Ashbury. She resolved to ask Lady Ashbury for the morning off so that she could accept the comtess's invitation.

Ushered into Mme. de Vaucouleur's tiny salon, Leonie felt a sense of chill from the moment she laid eyes on her hostess. The comtesse said distantly, favouring Leonie with the slightest inclination of her head, "*Bonjour*, mademoiselle. I trust you are well." Motioning Leonie to a chair, the comtesse sat down, her posture stiffly upright, her worn features an impassive mask.

After an uncomfortable silence, Leonie asked helplessly, "Have I offended you in some way, madame?"

"No, not at all," was the cold reply. "Your actions are of no interest to me, one way or the other."

"But then—I don't understand why you asked me to visit you. . ."

"That will be clear to you in due time. Ah—there you are, M. le Comte."

As Leonie rose, staring at him in shocked surprise, the Comte de Morville was shown into the salon by the elderly maidservant. He bowed deeply to each woman in turn. "Your servant, madame, yours, mademoiselle."

"I will leave you then, monsieur, to settle your business with Mlle. de Montbarey," said the comtesse, returning the comte's bow and sweeping past Leonie without deigning to look at her.

"Wait, madame, I have no wish to talk to. . ." Leonie's voice trailed away. The comtesse was already out of the room, the door closed firmly behind her.

Facing down the comte, trying to keep the apprehension that she felt out of her voice, Leonie said to him, "Obviously, you've poisoned Madame's mind against me. Just as obviously, you asked her to arrange a meeting here with you, knowing, I presume, that I would never have agreed to meet you voluntarily."

"That is quite true. Won't you sit down? I would like to talk to you for a moment."

"But I do not wish to talk to you." Leonie picked up her parasol, which she had leaned against her chair, and walked toward the door. "Please release my arm," she exclaimed sharply, as the comte put out a hand to prevent her from passing him.

"In a moment. After I have said what I came to say. It will only take a few minutes."

"Very well. I will listen to you. But please be brief," said Leonie reluctantly, knowing that she would lose all dignity if she struggled against the pressure of the comte's slim but powerful fingers.

"*Bon*. That is being reasonable." The comte released Leonie's arm, and she moved away from him with an unconcealed expression of distaste.

"Now, then, my dear Leonie, I would like very much to put an end to the unfriendliness between us. I am prepared to offer you a settlement of twenty thousand pounds and to buy you a house of your own choosing, either here in London, or in Italy. You might prefer to live there, at least for the time being. All this on your promise to remain with me at least five years—you see, I am a realistic man, and I know that all relationships change, or even come to an end. There now, what do you say to my offer?"

Leonie gasped. Twenty thousand pounds was an enormous sum, enough to enable her to live comfortably, even luxuriously for the rest of her life, but she spoke without a trace of hesitation. "I say no. I would not become your mistress for twice, thrice that amount."

"Think twice, *petite*. If the idea of living under my protection does not appeal to you—and quite frankly, I do not understand why—you may find that the alternative will appeal to you even less."

"What do you mean?"

"I mean, chérie, that Lady Ashbury might be distressed to discover that the governess to her young and innocent daughters was carrying on a clandestine affair with her own brother."

"There is no such clandestine affair," flashed Leonie angrily. "Mr. Deveril was kind enough to help me out of your clutches and to recommend me for a position with his sister, but that is the extent of our relationship."

"Really, my dear Leonie, you must take me for a complete flat," said the comte contemptuously. "I've known of Deveril for the past ten years, and I can assure you, he is no Galahad. But whether you have yet given in to him is beside the point. I'll wager that Lady Ashbury is completely ignorant of the circumstances in which you met him. And if you think that she would continue you in her employment once she knew of these circumstances, why you are far more simple-minded than I think you are."

"I don't have to listen to your threats. I bid you good-day." Leonie turned her back on him and started for the door. She stopped as the comte slipped past her to stand between her and the door. "I haven't finished yet," he snapped.

"But I have." With a lightning swift movement, Leonie raised her parasol and pushed hard at the comte's waistcoat just below his rib cage. When he doubled up—perhaps more from surprise than from actual pain—Leonie took advantage of his incapacity to wrench open the door and rush into the foyer, past the hovering maidservant and out into the street. There she paused for a moment, drawing deep breaths to calm her racing heart, casting an involuntary glance or two back at Mme. de Vaucouleur's house, even though she knew with the more sober part of her mind that the Comte de Moreville would never compromise his dignity to the extent of attempting to coerce an unwilling female on the open pavement. Then she walked briskly south on Baker Street, hoping to find a hackney cab at the juncture with Oxford Street.

It was fortunate for Leonie's peace of mind that she was completely occupied, the following day, with the Marlowe family expedition to Astley's Royal Amphitheatre. She had spent a nearly sleepless night, worrying about what the comte's next move might be, certain that he would spare no effort to ruin her life even though, after her rebuff, he might no longer desire her as his mistress.

She came down the steps of Ashbury House determined to put the machinations of the Comte de Morville out of her mind at least temporarily and to enjoy the outing that the young Marlowes had been looking forward to since their arrival in London. The children were already clustered around the two carriages at the curb, talking to Jeremy Deveril, who had volunteered to be, as he put it, the "bearleader" of the expedition. Leonie greeted Deveril with constraint; she had not seen him since the day that he had apologised for his behaviour at Granby Court, and she felt distinctly uncomfortable in his presence.

"Good afternoon, mademoiselle," he said. "I'm glad that you're accompanying us to Astley's. I told my sister that I might need a helping hand." He cast a rueful look at the group on the pavement, which included all the Marlowe children except Thomas and Lydia, plus a number of school friends of Edward and William. "When I told Edward and William that they might invite a friend or two, I never counted on this many. I daresay it would be very easy to lose one or several of them in a crush."

His manner was almost determinedly matter-of-fact, and Leonie told herself that she was happier for it. It was much safer for her to remain on the wariest of footings with Jeremy Deveril.

"I'm very happy to be included in the party, Mr. Deveril," she said quietly.

"I hope that you haven't misinterpreted my request to Lady Ashbury that you come with us," Deveril continued in the same formal tone.

"Misinterpret? I'm afraid that I don't know what you mean."

Was there the very slightest tinge of embarrassment in his normally self-possessed expression? Puzzled, Leonie studied him as he spoke, obviously reaching for words, "I mean to say, mademoiselle, that I hope you won't think that my request of today was meant to relegate you to the status of a—of a..." He paused.

"Of a paid companion? But that is what I am, Mr. Deveril."

Deveril flushed slightly. "You know that's not what I meant," he said in a low voice. "I simply did not wish to imply that I considered you to be merely a servant, regardless of your present necessity to earn your living."

Leonie flushed in her turn. She could assume that Deveril's remarks were an extension of his earlier apology to her, but she would not allow herself to speculate either on his motives for making this further effort, nor to examine her own feelings in regard to it. "I don't know what to say," she said after a moment, "except that I saw nothing at all untoward in your request to accompany you and the children today."

"Thank you." There was a faintly dissatisfied note in his voice, but he turned aside to shepherd his charges into the two carriages, his own town chariot and Lady Ashbury's open landau.

When the party arrived in Lambeth, Leonie was somewhat disappointed in her first glimpse of Astley's Amphitheatre, which on the exterior seemed to be a rather dilapidated structure with a canvas roof. But once inside the building, she was soon impressed by the sheer scale of the place with its three tiers of boxes surrounding the great sawdust ring, illuminated by an enormous chandelier holding fifty patent lamps and separated by the orchestra pit from London's largest stage, with a proscenium arch as high as the gallery above the highest tier of boxes. The Marlowe party had choice seats in the first tier, and the children settled down without the usual pushing and shoving, tittering and baiting, to wait in expectant silence for the superb equestrian acts and daredevil riding that had made Astley's famous throughout Europe.

Just before the performance started, Leonie, seated with Deveril at the rear of the box, was startled by the light touch of a hand on her shoulder. She looked up to see Thomas, accompanied by Robert Linton, sliding into place beside her. "No need to present you to Mademoiselle, Robert, you know each other very well," he said cheerfully. To Jeremy he said, "Uncle, I don't think you know my friend, Viscount Linton. Robert, my uncle, Jeremy Deveril." He smiled at Leonie. "No sooner did Robert hear that you were all going on this expedition than he wanted to come along, too. I knew you wouldn't mind. The more the merrier, is what I say."

Leonie was too upset by Robert's appearance to do more than barely acknowledge his presence. She glanced involuntarily at Deveril, and at his ironic, knowing gaze, she found her cheeks burning. Without a word on his part, she was certain that he was recalling his own wounding guess, during their first meeting, that Lady Linton had discharged her because of a suspicion that her stepson had become infatuated with the governess.

During the interval, Robert managed, to her discomfiture—Leonie suspected Thomas's connivance—to sit beside her. "Didn't I tell you," he said in a low-voiced triumph, "that I would contrive to arrange a meeting with you, if I put my mind to it?"

"And didn't I tell you that there was no reason for you to see me?" whispered Leonie furiously.

"Oh, but there is," said Robert simply, still in the same low tones. "Every reason in the world. I still love you. I want you to marry me."

"Be still, Robert. I won't listen to any more," hissed Leonie, resisting the temptation to jump up from her seat and leave the box. She glanced around quickly, to see if Robert had attracted notice to her by his attentions, but the children were buzzing excitedly about the magnificent riding they had just been watching. Only Jeremy Deveril was looking at her, and from the intensity of his gaze, she knew that he was aware of the nature of Robert's conversation.

Later, as they stood before Ashbury House, waiting for the children to be helped down from the carriages, Leonie went up to Deveril, saying, "I'm sorry that Viscount Linton intruded himself on your party. I knew nothing about it beforehand. I'm sure that Thomas extended the invitation impulsively."

"Think nothing of it," Deveril said carelessly. "As Thomas said, the more the merrier. I think that you should let young Linton know, however, that it is decidedly bad form for him to press his attentions on you so publicly," he added in a tone of slightly bored disinterest, giving Leonie the distinct impression that he was bestowing social advice on her somewhat reluctantly, purely from a sense of duty.

Leonie stared at him, her lips tightly compressed. Attempting to match his sang-froid, she said coolly, "I doubt that it will be necessary to speak to Lord Linton. I do not expect to see him again."

But in this Leonie was wrong. Returning from a walk with Amabel, Augusta and Charlotte several days later, she was hard put to control her annoyance when Robert Linton came up to them as they were turning out of Regent Street.

"Mlle. de Montbarey! What an unexpected pleasure to encounter you like this," he said blithely, removing the beaver hat that topped his newly modish curls and bowing deeply. "Lady Amabel, Lady Augusta, Lady Charlotte, your servant. May I accompany you for a little, ladies? It's such a lovely day for walking."

The three girls, dimpling and smiling, promptly invited Robert to join them, and Leonie realised, to her considerable surprise, that to them Lord Linton was a handsome, sophisticated Older Man. Inwardly seething, she said nothing to discourage Robert from walking along with them, biding her time until, having spent a few minutes with the girls discussing their thrilling experiences at Astley's Amphitheatre, he edged himself into place beside her at the rear of the little procession.

"You may have fobbed off your story on the girls," she said in a low voice, "but I don't believe for a moment that this was an accidental meeting."

Robert grinned. "Thomas told me that you walked almost daily with his sisters, but of course he didn't know what routes you followed. I've worn out a pair of shoes these past several days, hoping to see you."

Refusing to return his smile, Leonie cast him a quelling glance. "Robert, I hope that you'll listen carefully, when I tell you, one last time, that you must stop trying to see me. If you continue your attentions, you will cause me a great deal of embarrassment, and it's very likely that I will lose my position with Lady Ashbury, and, just as likely, that I would find it extremely difficult to obtain another post."

Her heart sank as she observed Robert's rapidly deepening look of mulish obstinacy. "It's you who won't listen," he insisted. "If you agree to marry me, there'll be no need for you to look for a position."

There was little point, Leonie told herself, in attempting to argue further with Robert, especially since the girls, their curious ears almost visibly extended, had been walking ever more slowly in an effort to overhear their conversation. In any case, they were just entering Cavendish Square, and, as they approached Ashbury House, Robert gave a little gasp at the sight of the carriage that had just come to a stop in front of the house. It took Leonie several seconds longer to recognise the crest on the carriage door; even as she did so a familiar figure was handed down the steps. Turning her head to glance at the group of walkers, Lady Linton's head remained fixed at an angle, as she stared at Robert and Leonie in frozen surprise. At length, without uttering a word, she turned to mount the steps of the house.

Robert's face was unnaturally pale. "I'd best come in with you," he muttered. "Mama isn't acquainted with Lady Ashbury, and this visit can only mean trouble."

"No, thank you, Robert," said Leonie with a firmness that she did not feel. "If there is to be any trouble, your presence here will only make it worse."

Leonie went straight to her bedchamber. She removed her hat and pelisse and quickly smoothed her hair, covering it with her usual demure cap. Then she sat down, clasping her hands in her lap, as she awaited the summons that she was sure would come. Within fifteen minutes there was a knock at the door. Lady Ashbury, said the footman, would like Mademoiselle to come to the drawing room.

Entering the room, Leonie went straight to Caroline, curtseying as she said, "You sent for me, Lady Ashbury?"

Her worn, pretty face looking very distressed, Caroline motioned to her visitor, saying, "I believe you are already acquainted with Lady Linton."

Leonie met Georgina Linton's hostile gaze calmly. "Yes, we've been acquainted for a number of years now. How do you do, Lady Linton? I trust your daughters are well."

Looking just as beautiful but somewhat less ethereal now that she was out of her mourning blacks, Georgina said coldly, "I would prefer to dispense with these empty formalities. May we come to the point, Lady Ashbury?"

Visibly upset, Caroline looked beseechingly at Leonie. "I am so sorry to subject you to this, mademoiselle, but Lady Linton has made some very serious accusations against your character, and I feel that it is only right to allow you the opportunity to reply to her personally."

"I have already told Lady Ashbury that I cannot agree with her position," cut in Georgina. 'I feel my word should be more than enough. I cannot, of course, dictate to her what she should do in her own house."

"May I know just what the accusations are that Lady Linton has made against me?" asked Leonie quietly.

"Well, my dear, she tells me, first of all, that she was very dissatisfied with the way in which you carried out your duties as governess to her daughters. However, since I have been more than delighted with your performance here, I do not consider your professional qualifications to be an issue. It's this other report that Lady Linton has brought to me..." Caroline broke off, her blue eyes filling with tears.

"Your distress is a credit to your sensibilities, Lady Ashbury," said Georgina. To Leonie she said, the note of triumph unmistakable in her voice, "Lady Ashbury is referring to the story told to me by the Comte de Morville, that you resided in his house for a period last summer as his paid—in the interest of delicacy, shall we say—paid companion? He is not proud of the association, you understand, but when he saw you in the company of Lady Lydia Marlowe in Hyde Park, he fell into a quandary, and asked for my advice: would it be honorable, he asked, to keep Lady Lydia's mother in ignorance of her governess's past history?''

"The comte is lying," replied Leonie instantly. "I accepted a position as governess to a young woman he called his niece. When I discovered that she was no such thing, that *she*, in fact, was his paid companion, as you put it, I left the comte's house. At no time was there anything improper between the comte and myself."

There was a bright spot of colour on both Georgina's cheeks. "The Comte de Morville is a friend of mine, and an honourable gentleman," she snapped. "I prefer to believe his story rather than yours, especially when I know you for a conniving wench who once tried to seduce my stepson."

"What a perfectly vile thing to say, Lady Linton," gasped Caroline.

"Vile perhaps, but quite true."

"It is quite untrue, Lady Linton," said Leonie. "I did my very best to discourage Robert's romantic notions."

"So you say," sneered Georgina. "If I had not discharged you, I daresay that you would have inveigled Robert to elope with you to Gretna Green. And now that you have unfortunately resumed contact with him, you're renewing your campaign to ensnare him. When the Comte de Morville observed you with Robert in Hyde Park, he realised at once that Robert was not at all surprised to see you. Later, Robert confided to him—my stepson feels the loss of his father acutely, and, I believe, has come to look up the comte as a wiser, older friend—that he had known for sometime that you were in London, and had cultivated Lord Thomas Marlowe in the hope of arranging a meeting with you. a meeting which finally occurred at Astley's Amphitheatre, Lady Ashbury, in the company of your own brother and most of your younger children! And finally, this very day, mademoiselle, as I was stepping down from my carriage in front of this house, I saw Robert walking with you and your young charges. Will you still deny that you have no interest in my stepson?"

"Is this true, mademoiselle?" faltered Caroline.

"Yes, the facts are true, but not Lady Linton's interpretation of them. If you will allow me to explain..."

Georgina rose. "I'll leave you to present to your employer what I'm certain she will perceive as perfectly futile explanations, mademoiselle," she said grandly, "the result of which will be that Lady Ashbury will no more require your services than I did."

Caroline stood. "You're mistaken, Lady Linton. I fully expect Mlle. de Montbarey's explanation to be satisfactory. I could not think ill of her."

"I can't believe my ears," Georgina retorted angrily. "Take the word of this slut over mine? Then all I can say for you is that you're both gullible and stupid."

Caroline was very pale. "I must ask you to leave, Lady Linton."

With a look of pure venom, Georgina inclined her head the merest fraction of an inch and swept majestically from the room.

After Georgina had left, Leonie observed closely Caroline's shaken expression, and realised with a flash of intuition that some of Lady Linton's barbs had shot home, despite Caroline's stout defense of her children's governess. She asked Caroline to sit down while she described in detail her experiences with the Comte de Morville. As Leonie talked, Caroline began to utter little sounds of sympathy and ended completely convinced of Leonie's innocence. When, however, Leonie shifted to the subject of Robert Linton, Caroline stopped her. "Oh, I don't believe a word of what Lady Linton said about your attempts to seduce her stepson," she declared roundly. "You see, my dear, I've noticed—though *some* people seem to think that I don't notice *anything*—that you managed to dampen Thomas's case of puppy love very diplomatically indeed."

"Oh," said a startled Leonie.

10

"MY DEAR, I just thought—I can't recall how long it has been since the fire lustres in the ballroom were taken down and polished..."

Leonie looked up from her list. She and Caroline were seated in the morning room, going over once again the preparations for Lydia's fancy dress ball. "The servants will clean the fire lustres tomorrow, Lady Ashbury."

Caroline was seized by still another alarming thought. "Lydia's costume—it hasn't been delivered yet..."

Leonie assured her employer. "The ball is still a whole week away. I'm sure the costume will arrive in plenty of time." She returned to her list, one of many she had made since taking over the management of Lydia's party. "We'll have one fewer guest than we had planned on," she remarked after a moment. "Lord Anderton sends his regrets—Thomas says the *on dit* is that the poor young man has caught the mumps!"

"Oh, dear, how humiliating," replied Caroline, unsuccessfully trying to repress a giggle. Turning thoughtful, she said, "You know how much I appreciate your help in arranging this ball, mademoiselle, but sometimes I feel guilty, letting you do so much of the work. Why, for the past week you haven't left the house at all."

"That has been entirely my own choice. It just seemed the safer thing to do, to avoid any chance of meeting Robert Linton. I don't care to provide Lady Linton with any more fuel for her dislike of me."

"I daresay," said Caroline uneasily. With a rush of candour, like a small child confessing to a breach of conduct, she blurted out, "I know you'll be most uncomfortable, my dear, but Thomas has just told me that he has invited Lord Linton to Lydia's ball. Really, I didn't know what to say to Thomas—one can hardly rescind an invitation."

Caroline looked so conscience-stricken that Leonie, with some difficulty, kept the dismay from her voice as she said, "Don't concern yourself about it. I won't be forced to see Robert, since I won't be attending the ball, and it's very possible that Lady Linton will never find out about it."

The morning room door opened, and Jeremy Deveril swept past the butler without giving that worthy an opportunity to announce him.

"I thought that you should know, Caroline," he began without preamble, "that I've just been summoned to the throne room for an interview that was remarkable for its sheer gall."

"I—I don't understand," faltered Caroline. "Do you actually mean that the regent...?"

"No, of course not the regent," snapped Jeremy impatiently. His normally imperturbable features were marred by a black scowl, and there was an angry electricity in his stride as he paced restlessly around the small room. "I'm referring to our own domestic imperial tyrant, Uncle Winchcombe. It seems that Georgina Linton, having failed to persuade you, Caroline, to discharge Mademoiselle, decided to acquaint the head of our family with her deeds." He stopped his pacing to stare accusingly at Caroline. "Why didn't you inform me that Lady Linton paid a visit?"

Caroline quailed. "I just—I just wanted to put it out of my mind, Jeremy."

"Well, I wish that you had told me. Forewarned, I might have looked less a fool in front of Uncle—will you believe that he told me I was criminally irresponsible to foist a woman of ill repute—probably one of my high-flyers, as he so delicately put it!—upon my sister's innocent children?"

"Jeremy!" cried Caroline, appalled. "He couldn't have said anything that dreadful—and that untrue!"

"He could, and he did. He also told me that he did not wish to see me until the matter—the matter, as if it were a tradesman's bill—was taken care of."

Caroline groped for her handkerchief. "What—what's to be done?"

"I can't tell you what to do, Caroline, but I'm much inclined to tell my lord the Earl of Winchcombe that he has no right whatsoever to dictate our conduct."

"Oh, but he would be so very angry," said Caroline, distress ravaging her delicate features. "He's promised to do so much for the younger children—Jeremy, couldn't you go to see him again when he's not quite so upset? Perhaps he didn't perfectly understand that Lady Linton was repeating lies told to her by the dreadful Comte de Morville..."

"That won't be necessary, Lady Ashbury," Leonie intervened. "I can't allow my presence here to endanger the futures of your children. I will leave immediately." She added, as Caroline opened her mouth to protest, "Please don't try to dissuade me. I know that what I'm doing is for the best."

Just then Lydia burst into the room, so wrapped up in her own affairs that she did not notice the air of gloom that had settled over her mother, her uncle and her governess. "Mama, can Mademoiselle go shopping with me this afternoon? Sarah Delaford told me yesterday that Wedgewood's—the linen drapers in York Street, you know—has some very pretty bugle trimmings and buttons."

"I'm sorry, Lydia, that I won't be able to accompany you," said Leonie quietly. "I will be leaving the house as soon as I can pack my belongings."

"Leaving us? You mean permanently?" asked Lydia incredulously. Then, attempting a strained smile, she exclaimed, "*I* know—you're just funning. That's it, isn't it?"

Caroline shook her head, sighing. "My darling, someone has gone to your Uncle Winchcombe with a disgraceful story about Mademoiselle. The story is quite untrue, but Uncle is furious about it, and Mademoiselle insists on leaving this house to spare all of us your uncle's anger. And much as I regret it, I think that perhaps she is doing a wise thing." Her eyes brimming with tears, Caroline looked at Leonie with a mute request for forgiveness.

Bewildered, Lydia asked, "What kind of story? I don't understand a word of this, Mama."

"I don't wish to go into it, my dear. Suffice it to say that your uncle became so enraged when he heard the story that he insisted to your Uncle Jeremy that Mademoiselle be dismissed. It isn't what I would wish, of course—I have absolute faith in her. But I need hardly tell you how much the family has come to depend on Uncle Winchcombe's generosity."

"So you're going to give in to him," Lydia burst out angrily. "Mama, it's grossly unfair that Uncle Winchcomb should have the power to make you dismiss Mademoiselle, all because of a lying story and after everything that she has done for us. Why, look at the hours she's spent organising my fancy dress ball, and now she won't even be here to see me in my costume."

"Lydia, I think you should apologise to your mother for speaking to her in that way," said Leonie, after she had recovered from the shock of seeing the ordinarily sunny-tempered girl fly into such a tantrum.

Lydia sniffed. "Oh, very well, I apologise, Mama. But," she added, flaring up again, "I still think that it's wrong to dismiss Mademoiselle. Uncle Jeremy, I'm sure that you agree with me."

The outward signs of anger had disappeard behind his usual aloof facade, but Deveril's face was very pale. "I fully agree with you about the injustice of the situation, Lydia," he said shortly, "and I'm more than willing to back up your mother if she chooses to defy our uncle."

"Thank you, Mr. Deveril, but I don't wish either you or Lady Ashbury to confront Lord Winchcombe on my behalf," said Leonie. She paused to think for a moment. Then, turning to Caroline, she said, "I haven't quite finished the final arrangements for the ball, Lady Ashbury. Would you like me to stay on for just a few days longer?"

Seizing on Leonie's offer with relief, Caroline said, "Oh, would you do that? I'll write to Uncle to say that you are leaving immediately. It won't be a lie, exactly, and besides, what he doesn't know will never hurt him."

"Mama, I have a glorious idea," cried Lydia, suddenly aroused from her gloom. "If Mademoiselle is only to be with us for a few days longer, I want her to come to my ball. Nobody would recognise her and Uncle would never hear of it—he never goes out socially."

"Why Lydia, what a strange idea," stammered Caroline. "I mean—that is to say, it's not customary..."

"You're quite right, Lady Ashbury," said Leonie, coming to Caroline's rescue. "One doesn't invite one's governess to a coming-out ball."

"But. . ." began Lydia mutinously.

"And besides, it's not correct to say that no one would recognise me," Leonie went on inexorably. "A great number of your friends saw me driving with you in Hyde Park."

"Pooh!" exclaimed Lydia. "Nobody ever really sees a governess."

"Lydia!" said Deveril sharply. "I won't allow you to speak slurringly of Mlle. de Montbarey."

"Pray, don't be angry with Lydia—I know exactly what she meant," Leonie cut in. She smiled at Lydia. "You may have a few faults—oh, a tiny one, or two!—but snobbishness isn't one of them."

Shooting a glance of triumph at her uncle, Lydia went on, "All I meant was that people don't see a governess as a person but as a—a type—you know what I mean, mademoiselle. And in the park you looked exactly like a drab little mouse with your plain grey dress and your bonnet that covered your beautiful hair." Renewing her attack, Lydia sat down beside her mother and said appealingly, "Please Mama—and you too, Uncle Jeremy—say that Mademoiselle can come to my ball. Don't you think that she deserves one night of pleasure before being driven away from us so cruelly?"

"My dear, I don't know," Caroline began doubtfully.

Deveril, his lips clamped firmly together over a still barely suppressed anger, suddenly snapped his fingers, saying, "Why not, Caroline? Lydia is certainly correct in saying that Mademoiselle deserves better of us. I think she would enjoy a ball into which she's put so much of her time and attention—and it would give me the satisfaction of knowing that we hadn't given in altogether to the family tyrant."

Lydia squealed in delight, and her mother, after a moment of uncertainty, said with unaccustomed firmness, "You're quite right, Jeremy. Uncle is being most unjust. Mademoiselle, you must come to the ball."

Leonie opened her mouth to remonstrate, but Lydia—as Thomas later described it—"rolled her up, horse, foot and gun," and dragged her from the room. "We'll go right to your bedchamber and plan your costume," she said, pulling Leonie up the stairs. "There's not much time, barely a week."

In Leonie's bedchamber Lydia chattered excitedly, throwing out one unlikely costume suggestion after the other. Becoming aware, finally, of Leonie's lack of enthusiasm, she said comfortingly, "I know you must be feeling so sad about going away from us, but I'm sure that Mama will find you another position, and very likely we'll be able to see something of you, once Uncle's anger dies down. I'll tell you one thing, I plan to hire you as governess to *my* children!"

Despite her gloomy mood, Leonie had to laugh at Lydia's artless attempts to cheer her. "I'd like that very much," she smiled, "but I hope you won't mind if I accept another position while I'm waiting for you to produce this family of yours. And about my attending your ball—it's lovely of you to want me, but it really isn't a very good idea. . ."

"It is, it is, and it's all settled. Or it will be, as soon as we've decided on your costume. We'll be going to the linen draper's this afternoon, and nurse could run something up quickly if it were simple enough, but. . ." Her brow furrowed in thought. Then her eyes fell upon the miniatures of Leonie's parents, and she exclaimed suddenly, "The very thing! You'll come to the ball as a belle of pre-Revolutionary France! Nurse can easily duplicate this dress your mother is wearing, and my maid could curl your hair in these big puffs, and we'll pinch some hair powder from one of the footmen. Oh, and my pink sash will look beautiful with the dress. The hat, now—that my be more difficult, but we'll manage somehow."

Picking up the miniatures, Leonie looked at the fresh young girl in the simple white gauze dress and wide-brimmed straw hat, and agreed that the costume would be easy to reproduce. She did not share Lydia's optimism that she would quickly procure another position—even if Caroline were to persuade a friend or acquaintance to offer her a post, Leonie feared that the lies spread by Georgina Linton would follow her wherever she went—but she tried to conceal her worries from Lydia, and, in the following days, she was caught up in the last-minute preparations for the party. She had to find whatever stray moments she could snatch for her own costume fittings when she was not supervising the laying of the carpet and the erection of the marquee in front of the house, arranging to engage extra servants and soothing the harassed cook, who showed ominous signs of an explosion at the news that a member of the royal family was expected to attend the ball. Leonie herself was somewhat apprehensive of her ability to provide for the needs of the Duke of Clarence, that good-natured sailor prince, who, she was told, was both exuberantly genial and foulmouthed.

On the night of the ball, Leonie put on her own costume before going in—for the last time, she thought rather wistfully—to dress Lydia's hair. After the maid had applied white hair powder to her own wide, elaborately curled coiffure, Leonie rather gingerly topped it with the large straw hat tied beneath her chin with pink satin streamers that matched the pink sash of the gauze gown, and stepped back to look at herself in the full-length "Psyche'—a pivoted looking-glass screen. She gasped as she looked from her image to the miniature of her mother on the dressing table. In every respect, the girl in the mirror was the exact duplicate of the young woman in the miniature. Except—Leonie reached for the small box that held her adoptive mother's few modest pieces of jewellery and took out the little pearl cross on a velvet band, the very same cross, she was sure, that her natural mother was wearing in the miniature. She slipped the cross around her neck and, after one last glance into the Psyche, left the room, her heart beating faster with a quite illogical feeling of excited expectancy.

When Leonie entered the room Lydia's toilette was complete—except for her hair—and though her Cleopatra costume was far from authentic, in Leonie's opinion she looked enchanting. As Leonie was adjusting the silver fillet around Lydia's tumbled curls, a knock sounded at the door and the chambermaid admitted Thomas. "I just came to see if your Cleopatra did my Marc Antony justice," he grinned. "I must say, you look much more comfortable, Lydia," he added, looking down at his heavy cuirass and leg greaves and the plumed helmet under his arm.

"You may not be comfortable, Thomas, but you certainly look very Roman," complimented Leonie.

He eyed her appreciatively. "I say, you are devilish pretty tonight. I know at least one person who will be bowled over to see you."

Glancing around hastily, Leonie was relieved to see that Lydia was busily engaged in gathering up her fan and reticule. 'If you're referring to Lord Linton," she said in a low voice, "I wish so much that you hadn't invited him to the ball. It's not fair to either of us."

"That's coming it a trifle too strong, mademoiselle. Robert will eventually discover that you haven't the slightest romantic interest in him, but in the meantime, what's the harm?"

Leonie looked sharply at Thomas. His statement that she was not interested in Robert Linton sounded completely matter-of-fact. She bit her lip, wondering if even the blithely unobservant Thomas had felt the subtle emotional undercurrents surrounding her and Jeremy Deveril.

After Thomas and Lydia had gone downstairs to station themselves in the receiving line, Leonie retreated to her bedchamber, having decided that she would not enter the ball until the middle of the evening, when her presence would be more likely to go unnoticed. Amabel, Charlotte and Augusta, who were manning their usual post at the head of the stairs, came in periodically to report on the arrival of guests.

"One lady was wearing the most peculiar headdress," said the awed Amabel. 'It looked like an enormously tall pointed cone with a veil attached to it."

"That was a hennin, Amabel. You remember, ladies in the Middle Ages wore them."

"Uncle Jeremy came as a Cavalier," chimed in Charlotte. "Or at least I *think* he's a Cavalier—he's wearing a wide lace collar and curled wig and plumed hat, anyway, just like the portraits in the picture gallery at home."

"You know, mademoiselle," said Augusta suddenly, "with your powdered hair you don't look like yourself, somehow. I'm not sure that I would know you."

Taking one last glance into the mirror screen before going downstairs, Leonie had to agree with Augusta; the powdered hair gave her an entirely different look, making her dark eyes and her delicate features seem much more pronounced. She left the room feeling less apprehensive than she had been that one of Lydia's guests might recognise her.

In the ballroom she was initially quite overwhelmed by the bright lights of the myriads of candles, the press of so many exotically clad people and the sheer volume of sound from the full orchestra. Finding a chair partially sheltered by a potted palm, however, she sat down near the entrance of the room, and soon she was enjoying the excitement and novelty of this glittering occasion that almost seemed, to her unfamiliar eyes, like something out of a fairy tale. She spotted Thomas, manfully struggling through a quadrille, and Lydia, flushed and smiling in the company of the dark and striking-looking Lord Manville. Caroline, not in costume, was seated at the side of the room, chatting animatedly with another dowager. A little later, she spied Deveril, poised and cool, about to lead out a partner for a country dance.

"There you are, Mademoiselle Leonie—Thomas told me that you wouldn't be down until later, so I didn't start searching for you until a few moments ago—and then I failed to recognise you. May I sit down?"

Leonie looked up resignedly at Robert Linton's smiling face. He was looking vaguely oriental in a satin tunic, draped trousers and a turban. "Yes, do sit down. You'll be less prominent sitting down than standing up. I daresay it will do no good for me to repeat that you shouldn't have come here, that your stepmother would be very angry if she found out about it."

Robert squared his jaw. "I don't care a whit if Mama is angry. She can hardly keep me on a leash or lock me up, you know."

"Please don't raise your voice, Robert. If *you* have no regard for your stepmother's opinion, I can assure you that I do. Are you aware that Lady Linton has just gone to Lady Ashbury's uncle, the Earl of Winchcombe, with a scandalous story told to her about me by the Comte de Morville? The earl—who, as you may know, is the great benefactor of the Marlowe family—became so angry after hearing the story that he ordered Lady Ashbury to dismiss me. I shall be leaving Ashbury House tomorrow."

Thunderstruck, Robert experienced difficulty in putting his words together. "Mama never said a word about this to me," he spluttered. "What kind of story are you talking about?

And what has any of this to do with the Comte de Morville?" He clenched his fists. "I'll tell you one thing, though—if Mama and the comte have really been spreading scandal about you to Lord Winchcombe, I'll insist on an immediate retraction!"

Leonie shook her head at Robert's well-meant incoherencies. "The nature of the comte's story isn't important. Nor would it do any good if the comte were to retract the story, supposing he could be forced to do so. The damage has already been done, I fear. I presume that Lady Linton didn't tell you about the comte's accusations because she feared that you wouldn't believe them, that they would probably make you more my champion than ever. You see, Robert, your stepmother is determined to break off any connection between us."

"Mama's instincts were right—I wouldn't believe a word against you!" snapped Robert.

"But don't you see, if you don't stop trying to see me, Lady Linton will only redouble her efforts to disgrace me?" Leonie pleaded. "I'll need to find another position when I leave here, and the least rumour of scandal will frighten off prospective employers."

Knitting his brows mulishly, Robert was about to continue his arguments, when a confident voice broke in.

"Mademoiselle, I've only just spotted you under that potted palm. Will you be so kind as to partner me in the country dance just forming?"

"Oh—thank you, no, Mr. Deveril. I hadn't planned to dance."

Deveril, dashing in his long curled wig and plumed Cavalier hat, raised an inquiring eyebrow. "Not dance? Why not, pray?"

"I don't think it wise to call attention to myself, Mr. Deveril."

Holding out his hand, Deveril said imperiously, "Nonsense, one comes to a ball to dance, not to watch. Come along, mademoiselle."

Almost without conscious thought, Leonie found herself walking across the ballroom floor on Deveril's arm. Why, she asked herself ruefully, had she gone against all her better instincts? Perhaps, she thought, she had merely wanted to get away from Robert's calflike importunities; perhaps she could not resist one venture into the heady fairy tale world of the *haut ton*; perhaps—she glanced sideways at Deveril's severely handsome features—just this one time, she had dropped her guard against the insistent magnetism that she had always felt between them.

As if reading her mind, as they took their places opposite each other at the end of the line, Deveril murmured, a glinting light warming his usually cold grey eyes, "I hope you realise that you're quite the most beautiful woman in this room."

Leonie coloured, dropping her eyes. "Please, Mr. Deveril," she said under her breath.

"I'm only telling you the literal truth, Leonie. Would you have me lie?"

Afterwards Leonie could not remember clearly a moment of the country dance. As if in a dream, she progressed to the head of the line and down again without missing a step, conscious only of Deveril's insistent gaze and the pressure of his hand on hers. As they were coming off the floor at the end of the dance, Lydia darted up to squeeze her arm and whisper in her ear that she looked perfectly beautiful. Leonie glanced across the room to find that Caroline was watching her with an affectionate smile; she returned the little wave of Caroline's hand and tears rushed to her eyes as she thought that tomorrow she would be leaving this lively, loving family.

"Is something wrong, Leonie?"

She shook her head. "It's just that—I suddenly realised how much I will miss Lady Ashbury and the children."

"But you're not cutting all your ties—you're sure to see us all again, some time," replied Deveril quickly.

"I can't let myself indulge in idle dreams, Mr. Deveril." The tears welled up afresh, and Leonie, surreptitiously wiping them away, said in a choked voice, "I should never have come down to the ball—I'll go up to my bedchamber now before everyone starts staring at me."

"Let me take you down to the library. We'll have a glass of wine while you collect your feelings," urged Deveril, taking her arm. They had just reached the doorway when they were confronted by a formidable figure who had just entered the ballroom.

"There you are, my boy," said the Earl of Winchcombe. "Parties are not at all in my line, as you know, but I decided that I would just look in for a moment on Lydia's fancy dress ball." As his gaze shifted from Deveril to his partner, the earl's wintry smile faded. Reaching slowly for his quizzing glass, he put it to his eye and stared fixedly at Leonie. After a long moment he lowered the quizzing glass, his face turning a purplish red; without saying a word he turned and strode stiffly from the room.

"*Mon Dieu*, he's recognised me," Leonie breathed despairingly. "Oh, why, why, did I allow myself to be persuaded to come to this dreadful ball?"

As if released from a momentary paralysis, Deveril took a few steps forward, calling out, "Uncle! Please wait!" But the earl, ignoring his nephew's voice, continued his majestic passage down the staircase. Deveril turned a harassed face back to Leonie. "I must go after him," he murmured. "I'll return as quickly as I can. Please don't fret yourself too much about this. I assure you, it's not the end of the world. Uncle strikes out at everyone and anyone when he flies into one of these passions, but I can generally bring him around."

Deveril's words were little comfort to Leonie, very conscious of the interested stares and lifted eyebrows of those near the ballroom door who had witnessed her encounter with the earl. Choking back a renewed flood of tears, she hurried from the room, down the corridor to the rear stairs.

"Mademoiselle, wait, please."

Leonie paused, her hand on the newel post. "Robert. I'm very sorry, but I can't talk to you now. Good night."

His young face drawn with anxiety, Robert reached for her hand. "I was watching you during your meeting with—that *was* the Earl of Winchcomb, wasn't it?—and I can see that something is terribly wrong. Leonie—Mademoiselle—please let me help."

"Nobody can help, I fear," said Leonie drearily. "A great calamity is about to fall on this family, and it's all my fault."

"A calamity?" echoed Robert. "I don't understand... There must be *something* I can do to help you—I can't bear to see you so unhappy."

"No, I thank you, it's very kind of you, but—" Leonie took a quick decision. "There *is* something—would you take me away from this house, immediately? Do you have your carriage here?"

Robert's face displayed an increasing bewilderment. "No, I don't. Mama was using the carriage tonight, so I walked here—it's only a short distance, you know. But I could go out and try to hail a cab..."

"No, that won't do." Leonie drew a deep breath, forcing herself to think calmly. "I was being very stupid. I can't pack up and leave here in the middle of the night, with a house full of guests and the children all wide awake upstairs, waiting for me to come up with cakes and tidbits from the supper tables. Could you come by for me tomorrow morning at first light, before even the servants are awake? I'll be waiting for you, just inside the door."

"Yes, of course, I'll do anything you ask," replied Robert promptly. "Where—where do you wish to go?"

Leonie looked blank for a moment. "I can't think—why, back to my former lodgings."

11

LEONIE PUT DOWN her pen and quickly read through the farewell letter that she had just written to Lady Ashbury. The bald words on the paper were totally inadequate to express the fullness of her feelings: her sorrow at leaving the family, her regret that the Earl of Winchcombe had seen her at the ball, her gratitude for Caroline's many kindnesses. But the letter was the best that she could do, and she hastily added a postscript: "The sooner I leave these premises, the sooner Lord Winchcombe will be able to put this sad situation out of his mind. Please don't worry about me—Lord Linton is coming to Ashbury House this morning to take me to my old lodgings with Mrs. Kirby. As soon as it may be convenient, please send on the rest of my belongings. Good-bye, dear Lady Ashbury—my thoughts and best wishes remain with you and your family."

Putting on her bonnet and her pelisse, Leonie gave one last look around her bedchamber, picked up her portmanteau, doused her candle and started down the staircase. It was still very early, just after sunrise, and none of the servants were yet stirring. Moving on tiptoe through the entrance hallway, she slowly pushed back the bolts on the door and slipped outside. As she stood at the top of the entrance steps, she felt both isolated and conspicuous, the only living creature in the vast silent square. Fortunately, her lonely vigil lasted for only a few minutes. Before she could begin to feel any strong anxiety, a carriage entered the square and stopped in front of Ashbury House. Eagerly she picked up her portmanteau and started down the steps as Robert Linton pushed open the carriage door.

"I knew I could count on you," Leonie breathed thankfully. "You're exactly on time. It would have been so awkward if any of the servants had seen me go."

"Is that all your baggage?" asked Robert, very businesslike. "Very well, then, let's get started." He handed Leonie's portmanteau to the neat, blue-uniformed postillion, and it was only then that Leonie noticed that several other pieces of baggage were already tied onto the brightly painted yellow carriage, which was, now that she looked at it closely, not a town vehicle at all, but a public post chaise.

"Robert, I thought you were going to use your mother's carriage," she began, when he interrupted her. "I don't like to waste time. Please get into the chaise and I'll explain later."

Confused, but as anxious as Robert not to be overtaken by the awakening daily routine of the square, Leonie allowed herself to be helped into the chaise. But as soon as the vehicle started up, she renewed her questioning.

"Really, Robert, a post chaise for such a short journey. I can see why perhaps you wouldn't wish to use your stepmother's carriage, but why didn't you just hail a hackney cab?"

"Well, I've been thinking. I don't believe that you should return to your former lodgings and just wait there until you procure another position. If Mama should persist in spreading her slanders—and I believe that she's fully capable of doing that—why, you would have little chance of finding another post." Privately Leonie had to agree with Robert's assessment. She had spent a largely sleepless night pondering what looked to be a very uncertain future. If Georgina Linton's vindictiveness did indeed follow her—and she could not find another position—her small hoard of money would last just so long, even with the most careful management, and after that... Wrenching her thoughts away from worrying speculation, she glanced out the window, noting that they had already turned into Oxford Street. But a moment later, when the chaise should have been making the turn south toward Piccadilly, it proceeded west, and, soon after that, turned north. She turned to Robert.

"We're not going to Mrs. Kirby's house in Piccadilly," she accused him. "Where are you taking me..." She thought suddenly of Robert's use of a hired post chaise and said incredulously, "You're not—you haven't taken it into your head to elope, surely?"

Robert crossed his arms stubbornly across his chest. "Yes. We're on our way to Gretna Green. There's nothing Mama can do to prevent our marriage in Scotland, even if I'm not yet of age. We can get married there without banns or license and Mama will just have to accept it. It will be a—what do you call it, a French something or other."

"A fait accompli," said the stunned Leonie automatically. They were on the New Road now, going north toward Islington, and all the while, as they drove past Somers Town and the brick kilns and factories and dairy farms of Pentonville and crossed the long lonely reaches of Finchley Common, Leonie tried unavailingly to persuade Robert to drop his harebrained scheme.

"I don't love you, Robert, surely you wouldn't wish to be tied for life to a woman who didn't love you," she pleaded.

"Perhaps you don't love me now, mademoiselle—Leonie—but you *are* fond of me. I'm confident that you will learn to love me."

Leonie threw up her hands. "Even if you were right, even if I did come to care for you, Lady Linton would never be reconciled to the match."

"We don't need Mama's approval. We can live happily without it," insisted Robert. "As I told you the first time I asked you to marry me, I have a small income from my grandmother—Mama can't touch that—and we can live modestly, if we must, until I come of age."

"Are you also prepared to live as a social outcast?" demanded Leonie "Because that's how it would be. Your stepmother will see to it that we—or at least I—will never be received in society." Briefly Leonie recounted to the horrified Robert the story of her entanglement with the Comte de Morville and Lady Linton's malicious misinterpretation of the facts. "So you see, Lady Linton, merely by speaking a few words into a number of carefully selected ears, could make sure that no respectable person would ever speak to me."

Even as Robert, after the initial shock, was feebly regrouping his forces—"I can't believe that even Mama would be such a monster, once we were actually married"—the chaise swept into the inn yard of the first posting stop at Barnet. Well aware that the efficient hostlers at the "Green Man" could change teams in less than five minutes, Leonie reached for the door handle, prepared to jump down as soon as the chaise stopped and dare Robert to force her back inside in full view of the crowded courtyard. She gasped in mingled anger and sheer incredulity as Robert seized both her hands and held her down forcibly until the chaise was once more under way.

"Never, never, lay your hands on me like that again!" she

choked. "If you do it again, I'll scream at the top of my voice—I don't care how embarrassed we'll both look."

The abashed Robert, more surprised at his own aggressiveness, perhaps, than even Leonie had been, dissolved into apologies. But he continued to insist, against all arguments, that no matter what obstacles Lady Linton put into their paths, marriage to him would be preferable to a return to governessing. At length, despairing of reaching Robert, Leonie lapsed into silence for the last few miles of this leg of their journey, intending to make a stand at the next posting stop. At Welwyn, however, before she could make a move, the landlord of the coaching inn thrust his head into the chaise as soon as it stopped.

"I'm very sorry, sir," he said, addressing himself to Robert. "We pride ourselves on our dispatch here, as I'm sure you know, sir, but I must beg your indulgence for a short delay—the chaise to which you were to transfer needs a slight—a very slight!—repair to one of its wheels. I'll have it fixed as soon as humanly possible, but in the meantime, won't you and the lady step into the inn to wait comfortably, perhaps have some refreshments?"

"Oh, very well," grumbled Robert. "I daresay it can't be helped."

The landlord, beaming, stepped aside and held up his hand to assist Leonie down from the chaise. Before Robert could get out, Leonie spoke sharply to one of the postillions. "Just leave my portmanteau out, please. Don't transfer it to the next chaise."

As the postillion gave her a look of sly speculation, Robert came up to her and murmured urgently, "Please, mademoiselle, give me one last chance to persuade you. Come into the inn—we'll have coffee and something to eat, I know you've had no breakfast—and then, if you still refuse to go with me to Gretna Green, we'll turn around and go back to London."

Leonie wavered. She *was* very hungry, she suddenly discovered, and returning to London with Robert in the post chaise would be far more comfortable than making the journey in the crowded public stagecoach. The thought of hot coffee won the day. "Very well. One last chance—and I have your word that you'll accept my decision."

In the cozy private parlour of the inn, over coffee and an appetizing light meal of cold meat, cake and bread and butter, Leonie was able to relax at last and even to feel that she was beginning to convince Robert of the wrong-headedness of his schemes, when she noticed that she was becoming sleepy. She glanced over at Robert, to observe that he too was having difficulty keeping his eyes open. The parlour door opened suddenly and she gaped in surprise at the sight of the tall, menacing figure of the Comte de Morville.

Robert leapt up from the table. "What are you doing here, you villain?" he demanded angrily. "This is a private parlour, you've no right to intrude on us. . ."

Advancing into the room, the comte eyed Robert with a careless smile. "So I'm a villain now, am I? I presume that Mlle. de Montbarey has at last confessed to you the details of our past—ah—close relationship."

His fists clenched, Robert started toward the comte, only to stop short when Morville produced a small pistol from his coat pocket. "Stay where you are, Lord Linton. I can box, of course—though I cannot understand the passion of you English for such a bourgeois sport—but my tastes don't extend to common brawling."

Frustrated, Robert could only glare at the comte as he asked sullenly, "I repeat, what are you doing here?"

The comte laughed. "My dear boy, you cannot expect to keep your plans secret if you must go into White's and Brook's well after midnight and attempt to borrow five hundred pounds. You collected the sum, finally, by cornering an assortment of your young friends, but one of them insisted on knowing why your request for a loan couldn't wait until morning, and you were forced to tell him that you meant to elope. He became very drunk later in the evening and told the story of your elopement as a delicious joke as he sat over cards with his cronies. I overheard him and guessed immediately who the bride must be. To get to Gretna Green, I knew that you would have to take the Great North Road and that you would change chaises at your second posting stop. So I drove here to Welwyn late last night and informed the host that I feared my young niece was about to elope. The innkeeper—all in the interest of family morality!—agreed to invent an imaginary repair to your chaise so that you would be obliged to step into the inn to wait out the delay. He also agreed to put a drug in your coffee so that I would have no difficulty getting my 'niece' to my carriage and so that there would be no unpleasant public scene with you, Lord Linton."

"You—you devil!" choked Robert. His eyes were unfocussed and his gait was shambling as he lunged forward, but he had taken only a few steps when he collapsed limply to the floor.

Her head was pounding, her mouth was very dry, and her eyes felt as if they were gummed together. Leonie forced her heavy eyes open and stared uncomprehendingly around her. She was lying on a bed in a small room that she had never seen before, furnished adequately but not luxuriously, and with heavy curtains drawn over the two windows. With great effort, for she began to feel nauseated as soon as she lifted her head, Leonie sat up on the edge of the bed and tried to force her befogged mind to concentrate. Suddenly she had a clear memory of poor Robert's drugged collapse, and she groaned as she recalled all the disastrous details of their "elopement" and ambush by the Comte de Morville.

Dragging herself off the bed, Leonie went to the room's

single door and tried turning the handle. As she had expected, the door was locked. She began a frantic battering at the door, shouting repeatedly for help. Soon the door opened, sending her half sprawling across the floor. The Comte de Morville entered, glancing at the elegant gold watch that he wore at his waist. "Awake at last, *petite*," he said approvingly. "I was beginning to fear that perhaps you had received an overly potent dose of the drug. You've been sleeping for almost twelve hours. It's very nearly midnight. Are you hungry?"

Panting, Leonie attempted to push past him through the door that he had left open behind him. He held her off easily, grasping her lightly with one hand as, overwhelmed by a sudden burst of nausea, she slumped limply against his arm. Carrying her to the bed, he put her down on the pillow, pulling a comforter up around her. "Stay there and rest awhile, chérie, until you feel more the thing. We'll talk later."

"Wait," said Leonie, supporting herself upright on her elbow. "Where am I?"

"You are in a private house that I have rented in Somers Town—you're not the first occupant, *naturellement!* You will have everything here that is necessary to your comfort and convenience—including a dragon of a housekeeper who will attend to all your needs and—most important of all—see that you don't escape. Because, make no mistake, chérie Leonie, here you will stay until you agree to become my mistress. I will be patient for a little while, until you make up your mind to accept my offer, but mark this, I won't wait too long."

"But this is kidnapping," said Leonie incredulously. "You can't seriously expect to keep me prisoner here indefinitely. Robert Linton will inform the authorities that you've made off with me, and then. . ."

The comte smiled. "It will be my word against Lord

Linton's. I have already paid the landlord of the inn a substantial sum to forget that we ever had any arrangement—he thinks that my desire for anonymity, *bien entendu*, is to protect my 'niece's' reputation. If Lord Linton's accusations ever trigger an investigation by the magistrates, why, then it will be even more to the interest of the landlord to forget that he had anything to do with the matter. But I daresay that once my investigators discover that young Lord Linton's light-of-love was once my mistress *en titre*, there will be an immediate loss of interest in your whereabouts. A dispute between two gentlemen over the favours of a beautiful courtesan is hardly the subject for an official inquiry. So, my dear Leonie, your good sense must inform you that there is only one way out of this situation for you. I'm going back to my own house now: I will wait for word from your 'housekeeper' that you have agreed to my terms. Don't keep me waiting too long."

After the comte had left the room, Leonie sank back against the pillow, a wave of despair combining with a renewed attack of nausea to plunge her into a black apathy that numbed her powers of reasoning. She closed her eyes, drifting off into a blurred state somewhere between sleeping and waking. Some time later, roused by the sound of angry expostulation below stairs, she propped herself up on her elbow, listening intently. Within moments, there was another sound, as someone began a determined battering at her door. One last crashing blow and the door burst open. Jeremy Deveril stormed in, brushing past the frightened harridan who made an ineffectual grab at his arm as he passed.

Rushing over to the bed, Deveril dropped on one knee beside it, inquiring anxiously, "Are you all right, Leonie?"

Leonie clutched his hand. "Yes, yes—I'm a little dizzy, but... Mr. Deveril, please take me away from here."

"That's what I'm here for. Here, let me help you get up. Where are your hat and pelisse—oh, here they are." Quickly and deftly, as if he were assisting a small child, he tied Leonie's bonnet under her chin and buttoned her pelisse. "Can you walk? Do you want me to carry you? No? Well, then, just lean on my arm and off we go."

"My portmanteau..."

Ordering the now subdued slattern to bring down the portmanteau, Deveril put his arm around Leonie and helped her down the staircase of the modest house, which was a near duplicate of all the small houses in Somers Town to which so many émigrés of modest means had swarmed on their arrival from Revolutionary France. As they emerged from the doorway, Leonie noted with considerable shock that dawn was just breaking; it was a full twenty-four hours since she had left Ashbury House with Robert Linton. Deveril's curricle, attended by his tiger, was drawn up in front of the house. As they drove of, Leonie's head began to clear. She filled her lungs with great gulps of the fresh early morning air. "How did you know where I was?" she asked wonderingly.

Deveril turned his attention briefly from his handling of the reins to flash her a grim smile. "It's been a very long day," he said, as he recounted the details of his search for her, beginning with his arrival at Ashbury House at nine in the morning with a request to see her.

"When I returned from attempting to talk to my uncle after he stalked out of the ballroom last night, you had already gone up to your room and I hesitated to disturb you at that hour."

"Was your uncle—Lord Winchcombe—very angry with me?" faltered Leonie.

Deveril's expression hardened. "I followed him out to his carriage and begged him for the opportunity to explain your presence at the ball, but he was thunderingly upset and brushed me off, saying he would discuss it with me today. So, first thing this morning I came to see you, hoping to reassure you, but my sister, very upset, informed me that Robert Linton had taken you to your former lodgings. I went straight to Mrs. Kirby's only to be told that you had never arrived there. So back I went to Ashbury House, where I had to put down a developing case of hysteria on the part of my sister and Lydia. Thomas, as concerned as any of us, suggested rather self-consciously that, since he knew Robert was very much in love with you, perhaps we ought to consider the possibility that you had eloped with him."

"I see," said Leonie. "And did you agree with Thomas that I might have eloped?"

"Heaven forgive me, yes," said Deveril. When Leonie, biting her lip, turned away from him, he placed one of his hands over hers. "I know now that you would never lend yourself to such a thing, but when I thought of the injustices you had already suffered at Lady Linton's hands, and reflected that she was just vindictive enough to pursue you indefinitely with her malicious lies, I could easily understand why you might think that marriage offered a way out of your difficulties."

"I see," said Leonie again. "That being the case, why did you chase after us? I presume that you did follow us, because otherwise you couldn't have known that the Comte de Morville abducted me."

"I followed you, my dear Leonie, because I was not going to allow you to marry Robert Linton," declared Deveril, with a finality that caused the clear colour to flood Leonie's cheeks. She freed her hands, saying, "How *did* you track us down? The comte informed me that he had bribed the landlord to swear that he, Morville, had never been near the inn."

"The worthy innkeeper's lies almost did throw me off the track," replied Deveril feelingly. "I knew the route Robert must be taking, of course—from London the only way to Gretna Green is via the Great North Road. At Barnet, the first stop, I learned that a young couple of your general description had changed horses there. At Welwyn, the same thing: the landlord told me—with rather more glibness than was necessary in retrospect—that the couple had changed into another chaise and proceeded north. But at Baldock the third stop, nothing. The obvious conclusion: either I was mistaken in the identity of the travelling couple, or Robert had no idea of eloping and had taken you to some destination in the countryside around Welwyn. Now, there, I knew I was on firm ground: you were not the girl to go aground in some love nest, nor was Robert Linton the man to persuade you to do so. I headed back for Welwyn, and, after a second talk with the landlord, realised that he was very uncomfortable about something. I was prepared to choke it out of him, but that proved unnecessary. My tiger, Jim, had been nosing about, chatting with the hostlers and the inn servants; one of the maids took him inside and whispered a story about the poor young man who had been taken so ill that very morning while—or so it was rumoured—he was on his way to Scotland to be married. I tore up the stairs right away, of course, to find young Linton just recovering consciousness and feeling sick as a dog. Pausing just long enough to send for a doctor and to put the fear of God into the landlord, I raced back to London to confront Morville in his own house in Mount Street. I will say this for the scoundrel, he's a tremendous actor: he acted surprised to see me, then puzzled, then outraged at my accusations. Lord Linton, he protested, must be imagining things, or even worse, he had injured or even killed Mlle. de Montbarey and was now trying to find a scapegoat for his crimes. He even offered to let me search his house, damn him!"

"And did you?"

"No. I knew you couldn't be there, or Morville wouldn't have made the offer. No, I grabbed him by the throat and threatened to keep choking him until he told me the truth."

Leonie experienced a moment of unreality at the thought of Deveril, that dandy among dandies, resorting to such violence.

"I don't think that our comte cares very much for physical contact," resumed Deveril, with a smile of pleasurable reminiscence. "He soon enough gave me the information that I wanted. He also challenged me to another duel, and I had to remind him that my marksmanship had, if anything, improved since last we met. I doubt that I will ever hear from his second. So, after relating all this excitement, Leonie, I fear that my story just runs downhill. I drove to Somers Town, brushed aside the dreadful old crone who was guarding you, and broke down your door."

Leonie shuddered. "I can never thank you enough. If you hadn't come as soon as you did—if only a day or two more had elapsed—I realise that no one would ever have believed that I was staying in that house against my will." She glanced around her, noting that they had turned down Baker Street. "Where are we going?" she asked.

"Why, back to Ashbury House."

"No, Mr. Deveril," Leonie said firmly. "I know Lady Ashbury's tender heart—once she learned of my abduction by the comte she would urge me to stay on. But my reasons for leaving Ashbury House are still valid: I can't allow Lord Winchcombe's disapproval of me to threaten the security of your sister and the children. No, I won't return to Ashbury House. Please take me to my former lodgings—if Mrs. Kirby will still have me, that is."

"Well, perhaps that would be better, for the time being," replied Deveril reluctantly. "And don't worry about Mrs. K.'s being willing to have you back. There will be no difficulty."

Which, indeed, proved to be the case. Leonie thought that she detected a slight shade of doubt in Mrs. Kirby's plump, kindly face as the ex-housekeeper plied her with questions about why mademoiselle had never arrived at the lodging house that morning as Master Jeremy had evidently expected her to do, but Deveril soothed her down with a smile and a pat on the shoulder and promised to tell her everything as soon as he had had an opportunity for a private chat with Leonie.

"Alone at last," grinned Deveril when the parlour door had closed on Mrs. Kirby's ample form. "Mrs. K. is the salt of the earth but she's never learned to stop talking."

"I—I don't understand why you wanted a private chat with me," said Leonie, a perplexed frown creasing her brow. "I thought that we had talked at some length on our drive here from the Comte de Morville's house."

"My darling girl, I'm not about to offer you a proposal of marriage while driving through the streets of London in a curricle," retorted Deveril. "I wanted to ask you last night—would you believe it, I suddenly realised while going down the line with you in the country dance that I was madly in love with you. Suddenly I knew that my evil temper of late, my gloom, my general discontent, were all caused by the prospect of never seeing you again."

Leonie stared at him, her eyes wide with shock. "You—you must be mad," she managed to say. "You can't possibly wish to marry me. Your uncle would certainly disinherit you at the first mention of such a plan."

"There's no way that my uncle could break the entail," Deveril said quickly. "Nothing he can do will prevent me from becoming the next Earl of Winchcombe."

Remembering Lydia's many confidences, Leonie shot back, "The bulk of your uncle's fortune is *not* entailed, however. And he's obligated only by his own good will to provide for your sister and her children."

Deveril walked over to her and grasped both her hands. "Are you telling me that you couldn't care for a much poorer man than you had anticipated I would be?"

"No, of course not," faltered Leonie. Her pulse had begun to pound at his nearness and there was a singing in her blood. "My feelings have nothing to do with it."

Deveril's face was pale and his usually hard grey eyes kindled with a soft, tender glow. "I can't believe my uncle would turn his spite on Caroline because of any anger he felt for me," he said tensely, "but even so, I cannot allow him to dictate what I should do in my own life. My darling, if you tell me that you don't love me and will not marry me, that will be the end of it. But if you do love me—if you only think that you might learn to love me. . ." He read the answer in her eyes, sweeping her close in a hard embrace, crushing her lips in a long, lingering kiss. With a little sigh, she relaxed against him, winding her arms closely around his neck.

Lifting his mouth at last, he looked down at her, his breath still coming unevenly as he said jokingly, "I'm so glad that you've stopped arguing with me, my love. I was beginning to fear that I was marrying one of those stubborn shrews who will never see reason."

At his word, Leonie suddenly wrenched herself from his embrace. She faced him resolutely. "I can't marry you, Jeremy. I simply will not be responsible for your being disinherited by your uncle."

Deveril shook his head in exasperation. "It's not even certain that Uncle *would* disinherit me. He's not a totally unreasonable man, and once we proved to him that Georgina Linton's tales were all lies, he could have no objection to my marrying a girl from an aristocratic French family. After all, his own wife, who died so many years ago, was French."

Leonie's mouth tightened. "There's the rub. I'm not at all sure that I come from an aristocratic French family. I really know nothing at all about my parentage, and I can assure you that your uncle would certainly object to that lack of knowledge." She put her hand to her forehead as she spoke, and

Deveril, sensing her weariness and nervous strain, said, "We'll talk about it another time, my love. Right now I'm going to ask Mrs. K. to give you some tea and perhaps some soup and then tuck you into bed for a long rest." He lifted her chin, kissing her gently, and left the room.

Listening to his voice talking to Mrs. Kirby in the corridor outside, Leonie felt all her defenses dissolving and broke into a storm of tears. When Mrs. Kirby came into the parlour, she expressed no surprise at Leonie's emotional state, but planted a comforting arm around her shoulder and bustled her out into the kitchen.

12

"Visitors to see you, Miss Leonie."

Putting aside her needlework, Leonie stood up. Keenly aware of her erratically racing pulse, she could not decide, as she gazed at Jeremy Deveril's tall figure behind Mrs. Kirby at the entrance to the parlour, whether she was more glad than sorry to see Deveril again, so soon after the tumultuous events of yesterday.

"Mr. Deveril, I really don't think this is wise," she began, when he cut her short, crossing the room to her and placing a protective arm around her as he faced his uncle, who had entered the room directly behind him.

"Lord Winchcombe!" exclaimed Leonie, turning pale and shrinking back against Deveril's arm.

"Pray don't be alarmed, mademoiselle," said the earl. "I would like to tender you my apologies for causing you any anxiety by my behaviour at my niece Lydia's ball. And I would like very much to talk to you briefly, if you will favour me with your permission."

Puzzled, Leonie looked for enlightenment to Deveril. He shrugged, sending a challenging glance in his uncle's direction as he said, "I've again told Lord Winchcombe that Lady Linton's accusations against you are outright lies. *And* I've told him that my heart is set on marrying you. He insisted on accompanying me here this morning."

Catching her breath, Leonie gazed apprehensively at Lord Winchcombe and was surprised to discern no noticeable reaction to Deveril's announcement. There seemed in fact, to be an attempt at a rather wintry smile on his mouth as he said, in his old-fashioned courtly way, "Will you sit down, mademoiselle?"

There was a long pause, during which Leonie began to feel decidedly unnerved, as the earl turned upon her a silent, probing stare, almost as if he were analysing her features one by one. He broke the silence by asking, "May I ask where you got the inspiration—if, indeed, anywhere—for the costume that you wore at Lydia's ball?"

The question, so totally unexpected and so seemingly irrelevant, momentarily nonplussed Leonie. "Why, I simply copied a dress worn by my mother in a miniature painted of her when she was a very young woman," she replied after a moment.

"I see," said the earl, slowly clenching his fists. "May I see it?"

"Yes, certainly." Leonie rose to leave the room, glancing back at Deveril in deepening puzzlement. She quickly went up to her bedchamber, snatched up the miniature and hastened down the stairs. She handed the miniature to the earl and sat down again next to Deveril.

The slow minutes ticked away as the earl, scarcely moving a muscle, sat hunched over the painting of the young girl in the simple white dress, her powdered curls topped by an airy straw hat. Looking up finally, he said to

Leonie, "My nephew informs me that you are an adopted child. Please believe me when I tell you that I am not being merely curious—could you tell me something of your background?"

More uncomprehending than ever, Leonie glanced at Deveril, who merely raised a puzzled eyebrow. "I don't know very much, really, about my background," she said slowly. Briefly, she went on to sketch for the earl the bare outline of her adoptive parents' meeting with the young woman of the miniature at the boarding house in Rotterdam. "My parents only saw Mme. de Mirecourt—as she was called—when she was already comatose. Fellow lodgers told them that the young woman was very ill when she arrived in Rotterdam with her baby, and they assumed, since she was dressed in deepest black, that her husband had been killed fighting with the Army of the Princes at Valmy. In a letter written before he died, my adoptive father told me that Mme. de Mirecourt cried out in her delirium that she wanted to join her husband, whom she called Leonard, and my parents assumed that she meant that she wished to join him in death. And that, Lord Winchcombe, is all that I know about my real parents. I was named Leonie, after my presumed father, and I have some miniatures—the painting you have in your hand, and a likeness of the man I believe to be my father—and a locket, all of which were in my mother's possession, but I have no other clue to her identity."

"You have another miniature?" asked the earl quickly. "Could I see it, please?"

Leonie made another visit to her bedchamber, and as she sat watching the earl, bent in painful concentration over the second miniature, she suddenly had a flash of illumination. "I think I begin to see why you are so interested in these miniatures, sir. Could it be—could it possibly be—that you recognised me from my resemblance to a lady you once knew? Do you know who my real parents actually were?"

There was an odd smile on the earl's lips as he reached over to place her father's miniature in Leonie's hands. "Look at the pair of us closely, my child. Do you see any resemblance?"

Increasingly bewildered, Leonie studied the painted face in the miniature, with its strong features and searching blue eyes, and then looked up to scan the lined, haggard face opposite her. Her eyes widened as she slowly realised that, allowing for the marks of suffering and disillusion and the changes wrought by time in Lord Winchcombe, the two faces were identical. She was overcome, and could barely form her next question. "Are you telling me," she gasped, "that *you* are my father, sir?"

The earl nodded. His eyes were bright with unshed moisture as he said, "Yes, *ma chére* Leonie, I'm your father, Leonard Deveril—did you note my Christian name? Dressed as you were at the fancy dress ball, you were the image of your mother as I first knew her. I was so overwhelmed at the resemblance, so thunderstruck, that I could not speak of it at the time. I turned around and left the house, trying to sort out my thoughts, wondering if the resemblance was merely coincidental, agonising over the possibility that I had found the child who I had always believed had died in her mother's womb. I came back the next day to Lady Ashbury's house, determined to search out the truth, only to be told that you were gone." He stood up, stretching his arms. "My dearest little girl, will you let me claim you as the daughter that I never knew I had?"

Hesitating not a moment, her grief at discovering that she was not the Montbarey's natural child dissolving like snow in a warm spring rain, Leonie rushed into her father's arms, to be held tightly in a sheltering embrace that she felt instantly to be natural and inevitable. Moments later, she and the earl were aroused from their blissful daze by Deveril's voice commenting incredulously, "My God, Leonie, so your name is really Deveril and you've turned out to be my cousin?"

Relaxing his embrace, but still retaining an arm around Leonie's shoulder, the earl cleared his throat, looking somewhat self-conscious at his display of public emotion. "It's a very distant relationship, nephew. Your grandfather was my first cousin, which make you and my daughter, by my reckoning, second cousins once removed."

Leonie looked up at the earl, her face wreathed in a shy but radiant smile. "Won't you sit down, *mon père*, and tell me something about my mother and your life together? There are so many things I long to know."

Some of the joyful glow faded from the earl's face and there was a definite strain in his voice as he began his account. "Your mother's name was Françoise," he said to Leonie. "She was the daughter of the Comte de la Coulommiers, who had estates in Orléans near St. Benoît. She was a beautiful girl, eighteen years old, with brown eyes and lovely red-gold hair. When I met her, I was much older—in my mid-thirties—and I had no special desire to settle down in marriage. But I fell in love with Françoise the moment I set eyes upon her, and immediately asked for her hand in marriage. Her parents told me that she had had a romantic attachment to a cousin, but the match was considered unsuitable because of the closeness of the blood tie—and also, I gather, because the cousin had very little fortune—and was broken off. In those days, of course, even more so than in our time, romantic affection was not considered necessary, or even desirable in marriage, and Françoise seemed perfectly willing to accept my offer, once her parents indicated their approval. We were married a short six weeks after we first met."

The earl paused, the strain in his voice more evident. It was obviously that this normally cold and impassive man found it difficult to speak about his most private emotions. "The marriage was very happy at first—or at least I thought it was, until I began to perceive that Françoise's affection for me was much less deep than mine for her. You will think, and quite rightly, that my feelings were illogical, but then logic has very little to do with emotion. I became increasingly unhappy, and, I'm sure, increasingly miserable to live with. Then, in August of 1789, as one of the Prince of Wales's aides, I went off with him on a long holiday to visit various friends of the prince in York. When I returned to London some weeks later, I found that a young relation of the Coulommiers family was visiting Françoise. To this I naturally made no objection, until I discovered that, not only was Françoise pregnant, but the visiting relation was the selfsame cousin with whom she had been in love before her marriage. I flew into a blind rage, accused Françoise of adultery and her cousin of fathering Françoise's child, and challenged the cousin to a duel. I was an excellent shot, he was not. He died of a bullet wound in the chest. Immediately after the funeral Françoise left my house. She left a letter saying that she had never been unfaithful to me, that her expected child was indeed mine, that she had long ceased to feel more than a family affection for her cousin, but that she could no longer live with a man who was capable of killing a fellow human being in a jealous rage. Her father wrote to me shortly afterwards, telling me that Françoise had fled to her parents' home; he and his wife were insisting that Françoise carry out her marital duties, and they asked me to come to France to escort her home to England."

Pausing again, the earl looked at Leonie with a hint of

desperation, as if he feared her adverse judgement on his long-ago actions. "God forgive me," he went on, "in my bitterness and—yes, self-hatred—I was a long time coming to accept the truth of Françoise's innocence and longer still to acknowledge that I had forced a duel upon an equally innocent man. It was late October before I decided to go to France to bring my wife home. I was aware, naturally, that there had been a revolution in the country—in fact, in common with many in the Prince of Wales's circle, I had followed the events closely. But I had assumed that, with the end of the great peasant uprisings in July, France was once more at peace. On arriving in Orléans, I was totally unprepared to find that a local insurrection had destroyed the Coulommiers estate and that everyone in the family had been killed. We will never know what actually happened, of course, but I think that I can explain how Françoise escaped the massacre of her family: I believe that she was reluctant to return to me, and, on being informed by her parents that I was on my way to fetch her, she fled from her parents' home and sought refuge elsewhere, probably with a favourite uncle who had property in Lorraine near Mirecourt—your mother's use of the name Mirecourt rather substantiates that."

Leonie's expression was intent and sadly pensive, but not condemning. "And then, as the situation in Lorraine became more and more violent, my mother probably escaped to Coblentz with the other Royalists and thence to Holland, after the defeat at Valmy," she said after a moment.

The earl nodded. "It seems likely," he agreed. "I would guess that her resources were exhausted by that time and that she had decided to ensure her child's safety by returning to England—and to me." He added, half under his breath, "That, too, is something I will never know, but I will continue to hope that it was more than sheer expediency—that Françoise had also found it in her heart to forgive me."

Rising, Leonie crossed to her father's chair, placing her arms around his shoulders and resting her chin on his thick hair. "I'm, sure that she did, *mon père*," she murmured. "Don't you remember what my foster father told me in his letter, that my mother, in her last delirium, spoke of joining you?"

The earl reached up to place one of his hands over hers. "Thank you for reminding me, my dear," he said with a catch in his voice. Clearing his throat again, he fixed a stern eye on Deveril, saying, "Well, now, young fellow, all this will make a vast difference in your situation."

"What do you mean, sir?" asked Deveril blankly.

"Why, quite simply, that your expectations are vastly changed. My daughter will now become my principal heiress. So, while you will succeed me as Sixth Earl of Winchcombe, you will come into the title with only a modest income to sustain the estate. You now occupy, therefore, a much lower place in the matrimonial market place.

Deveril rose, staring at his uncle with such cool hauteur that Leonie, despite her distress at what her father seemed to be saying, could barely restrain a smile. The two men, so far apart in age, wore nearly identical expressions of confident arrogance. "Are you telling me, sir," Deveril demanded, "that you are opposed to my marrying your daughter?"

Putting Leonie gently aside, the earl rose in his turn. "I'm telling you, my boy, that my only wish is for Leonie to be happy. She may marry whomever she likes, though I hope that she won't marry anyone for a year or two. I would like her to stay with me until we have made up for the lost years. I will venture to suggest to her, however, that, as the greatest heiress in England, she might choose to look a little higher for a husband than an impoverished earl. With her fortune and her beauty she could be a duchess tomorrow."

Deveril picked up his hat, bowing first to Leonie and then to the earl. "If you include the Continent, Lady Leonie could as easily be a princess," he said coldly. "But that, of course, is entirely up to her. I will bid you good day."

He was halfway to the door when Leonie cried out, "Jeremy, don't go!"

He turned around slowly. "Well, Leonie?"

Lifting her chin and straightening her shoulders, Leonie faced the earl. "I'm sorry to displease you, *mon père*, but I have no desire at all to be a princess, or even a duchess. I'm going to be the Countess of Winchcombe, if Jeremy still wants me. And if you don't choose to make either of us your heir, I suggest that you leave your money to a worthy charity. No doubt my friend, the Comtesse de Vaucouleurs, could give you the names of vast numbers of deserving poor French émigrés!"

She braced herself for an explosion from her formidable parent but the earl merely smiled. It was a rather forced, feeble smile, from a man who for these many years had had little occasion to smile, but it was a smile nevertheless. "Certainly, *ma fille*," he said affably. "I have already told you that you could marry whomever you like, recall. I merely wanted to make sure that you didn't allow yourself to be swept into marriage with my nephew because you felt that his—your—family thought it suitable, or desirable. I repeat, you can have your pick of the marriage mart. And now, I am going to take my leave of you temporarily. I've been staying in a hotel for what I thought would be only a brief stay in London, but now I'm off to arrange to have my town house opened. Deveril, I know that I can depend upon you to take Leonie and her belongings to Ashbury House, until I can prepare her own home for her." He dropped a kiss on Leonie's forehead and strode from the parlour. As the door closed behind him, Deveril broke into a chuckle. "I thought my revered uncle was doing it rather too brown," he grinned. "But I was caper-witted enough to believe—just for an instant—that he really was opposed to our marriage."

"Do you mean that he was just—just funning?"

"Oh, yes. I think he was so full of unexpected happiness that he felt rather like a bottle of champagne about to pop, and he was simply getting rid of some of his excess spirits at my expense. You must realise, my love, that your father is making up for years of unrelieved gloom! But I would stake my blunt that he has every intention of seeing us happily wed."

"Oh." Leonie looked away. "Our marriage is just a foregone conclusion, then? A good idea to keep me—and my money, too, probably—in the family?"

"Leonie!" Deveril grabbed her by her shoulders. "Of course I didn't mean—I thought that you loved me..."

Leonie held him off. "I just realised that we haven't talked at all about—about our feelings. When did you know that you loved me, Jeremy? Did the knowledge hit you like a bolt of lightning at Lydia's ball?"

The laughter had left Deveril's face and his expression was deadly serious, with just a hint of uncertainty detracting from his usual superb confidence. "I don't know when I started to love you," he said slowly. "You were always partially right, when you accused me of presuming upon my position. Gentlemen don't usually marry governesses! But after you went down to Granby Court to begin teaching my nieces, I noticed that your face kept intruding into my thoughts, so I went to my sister's house to spend a long Christmas holiday. My nieces must have told you—they can't keep their tongues still about anything else—that I normally stay at Granby Court for only a few days, at the end of the Christmas season."

"Oh, they did tell me, but they had a perfectly rational

explanation for your early arrival," said Leonie kindly. "They said you wanted to spend more time in Lady Selena's pocket, and I must say, you did ride over the Cartwright estate several times a day."

Deveril's fingers tightened on Leonie's shoulders. "I never gave a thought to Selena from the day I kissed you, after you fell off that miserable horse at Granby Court. And from then until Lydia's ball, I found that I couldn't stop thinking of you. I even—I admit it freely—wondered once or twice if I should ask you to become my mistress. No, Leonie, listen to me," he ordered, as she attempted to wrench herself away from him. "I swear to you, I never considered it seriously. I always knew that for you it could never be a possible choice. And then, when we danced together at Lydia's ball, I realised in one blinding flash that I wanted you for my wife, that I wanted to spend the rest of my life with you." He folded his arms more closely around her, looking down at her with kindling eyes. "When did you know about us, Leonie? For I'll swear, you feel the same as I do."

Leonie felt the tingling glow of colour suffusing her cheeks, but she kept her eyes fixed to his as she said softly, "I think that I've been fighting against my feelings for you since the first day that we met."

Drawing a quick, ragged breath, Deveril crushed her to him, claiming her lips in a long bruising kiss. When at last he lifted his head, the fitful gleam of passion still played in his eyes, and he said huskily, "When will you come to me, my darling Leonie? How soon can we be married?"

Leonie shook her head doubtfully. "I think that I must stay with my father for a while, dearest. It would be cruel to leave him alone so soon after finding each other at last. But oh, Jeremy, the waiting will be just as hard for me as it is for you."

Deveril rested his face against her hair as he cradled her in his arms. "I'll wait because I must, love," he murmured. "But every moment of waiting will be an agony until the day when you belong to me, completely and forever.

Superb Romances
from REBECCA BRANDEWYNE

___ LOVE, CHERISH ME *(D34-220, $4.95, U.S.A.)*
(D34-221, $5.95, Canada)

"Set in Texas, it may well have been the only locale big enough to hold this story that one does, not so much read, as revel in. From the first chapter, the reader is enthralled with a story so powerful it defies description and a love so absolute it can never be forgotten. LOVE, CHERISH ME is a blend of character development, sensuous love and historic panorama that makes a work of art a masterpiece."
—*Affaire De Coeur*

___ NO GENTLE LOVE *(D30-619, $3.95, U.S.A.)*
(D32-136, $4.95, Canada)

She was a beauty, besieged by passion, sailing from Regency, England to mysterious Macao on an unchartered voyage of love. She was also unready to accept love in her heart for the domineering, demanding man whose desire for her was jealous, violent, engulfing, but enduring.

___ FOREVER MY LOVE *(D32-130, $3.95, U.S.A.)*
(D32-131, $4.95, Canada)

They were born to hatred, but destined to love. Echoing across the stormy waters of Loch Ness came a gypsy's haunting curse, foretelling a forbidden passion that would drench the Scotish crags with blood. And from the first moment that Mary Carmichael lifted her violet eyes to those of Hunter MacBeth, the prophecy began to come true. Theirs is a legend of struggle against relentless hate, of two wild hearts who pledged defiantly FOREVER MY LOVE.

___ ROSE OF RAPTURE *(D30-613, $3.95, U.S.A.)*
(D32-724, $4.95, Canada)

She was an orphan and had been protected since childhood by the Duke of Gloucester, who would be called King Richard III by all Englishmen—and murderer by some. And she would discover that those who accepted the king's kindness must share his battles, though the blood might run as red as the rose that was the emblem of his enemies . . .

Her name was Lady Isabella Ashley. For her love, men schemed and struggled as fervently as they battled for the throne of England. They called her Rose of Rapture.

WARNER BOOKS
P.O. Box 690
New York, N.Y. 10019

Please send me the books I have checked. I enclose a check or money order (not cash), plus 50¢ per order and 50¢ per copy to cover postage and handling.*
(Allow 4 weeks for delivery.)

_____ Please send me your free mail order catalog. (If ordering only the catalog, include a large self-addressed, stamped envelope.)

Name _____
Address _____
City _____
State _____ Zip _____

*N.Y. State and California residents add applicable sales tax.

Passionate Reading from VALERIE SHERWOOD

___THESE GOLDEN PLEASURES (D30-761, $3.95)

She was beautiful—and notorious and they called her "That Barrington Woman." But beneath the silks and diamonds, within the supple body so many men had embraced, was the heart of a girl who yearned still for love. At fifteen she had learned her beauty was both a charm and a curse. It had sent her fleeing from Kansas, had been her downfall in Baltimore and Georgia, yet kept her alive in the Klondike and the South Seas.

___THIS LOVING TORMENT (D32-831, $4.95, U.S.A.)
(D32-832, $5.95, Canada)

Perhaps she was *too beautiful!* Perhaps the brawling colonies would have been safer for a plainer girl, one more demure and less accomplished in language and manner. But Charity Woodstock was gloriously beautiful with pale gold hair and topaz eyes—and she was headed for trouble. Beauty might have been her downfall, but Charity Woodstock had a reckless passion to live and would challenge this new world—and win.

___THIS TOWERING PASSION (D30-770, $3.95)

They called her "Angel" when she rode bareback into the midst of battle to find her lover. They called her "Mistress Daunt" when she lived with Geoffrey in Oxford, though she wore no ring on her finger. Whenever she traveled men called her Beauty. Her name was Lenore—and she answered only to "Love."

___HER SHINING SPLENDOR (D30-536, $3.95, U.S.A.)
(D32-337, $4.95, Canada)

Lenore and Lenora: their names are so alike, yet their beauties so dissimilar. Yet each is bound to reap the rewards and the troubles of love. Here are the adventures of the exquisite Lenore and her beauteous daughter Lenora, each setting out upon her own odyssey of love, adventure, and fame.

WARNER BOOKS
P.O. Box 690
New York, N.Y. 10019

Please send me the books I have checked. I enclose a check or money order (not cash), plus 50¢ per order and 50¢ per copy to cover postage and handling.*
(Allow 4 weeks for delivery.)

_____ Please send me your free mail order catalog. (If ordering only the catalog, include a large self-addressed, stamped envelope.)

Name _____

Address _____

City _____

State _____ Zip _____

*N.Y. State and California residents add applicable sales tax.

You'll also want to read these thrilling bestsellers by *Jennifer Wilde* ...

__LOVE'S TENDER FURY (D32-813, $4.50, U.S.A.)
(D32-814, $5.50, Canada)

The turbulent story of an English beauty—sold at auction like a slave—who scandalized the New World by enslaving her masters. She would conquer them all—only if she could subdue the hot unruly passions of the heart.

__DARE TO LOVE (D32-746, $4.50, U.S.A.)
(D32-745, $5.50, Canada)

Who dared to love Elena Lopez? She was the Queen of desire and the slave of passion, traveling the world—London, Paris, San Francisco—and taking love where she found it! Elena Lopez—the tantalizing, beautiful moth—dancing out of the shadows, warmed, lured and consumed by the heart's devouring flame.

__LOVE ME, MARIETTA (D30-723, $3.95, U.S.A.)
(D30-762, $4.95, Canada)

The enthralling come-back of Marietta Danver, the provocative heroine of LOVE'S TENDER FURY. Her beauty was power ... men fought to touch her, hold her, and staked claim to her body and her heart, men beseeched her, but Marietta Danver would keep her love for just one man!

WARNER BOOKS
P.O. Box 690
New York, N.Y. 10019

Please send me the books I have checked. I enclose a check or money order (not cash), plus 50¢ per order and 50¢ per copy to cover postage and handling.* (Allow 4 weeks for delivery.)

_____ Please send me your free mail order catalog. (If ordering only the catalog, include a large self-addressed, stamped envelope.)

Name _____
Address _____
City _____
State _____ Zip _____
*N.Y. State and California residents add applicable sales tax.

Especially For You from JANET LOUISE ROBERTS

__FORGET-ME-NOT *(D30-715, $3.50, U.S.A.)*
(D30-716, $4.50, Canada)

Unhappy in the civilized cities, Laurel Winfield was born to bloom in the Alaskan wilds of the wide tundras, along the free-flowing rivers. She was as beautiful as the land when she met the Koenig brothers and lost her heart to the strong-willed, green-eyed Thor. But in Alaska violence and greed underlie the awesome beauty, and Laurel would find danger here as well as love.

__GOLDEN LOTUS *(D81-997, $2.50)*

She was reared with delicacy in a Japanese-American family. He was tough, competitive, direct. Could she love him when he made her feel more like a prized possession than the woman he needed? Could he ever make her understand the depth of his love? Their marriage is a passionate struggle that will revolve itself in either ecstatic triumph or rejection.

__SCARLET POPPIES *(D30-211, $3.50, U.S.A.)*
(D30-677, $4.50, Canada)

Beautiful designer Iris Patakos had fulfilled her dream of a career in the fashion capital of the world. But a wealthy, powerful stranger was to sweep her from New York City to the opulent splendor of the Greek isles. Gregorios Venizelos, whose eyes blazed with black fire, had stolen the heart Iris had vowed never to give.

__FLAMENCO ROSE *(D95-583, $2.75)*

She was Rosita, the Flamenco Rose. A gypsy dancer whose dark-haired beauty pirouetted her to fame in the world of ballet. But Rosita yearned to control her own destiny, even if it meant defying her wild heritage, her demanding mentor, and the passionate, possessive man she loved.

WARNER BOOKS
P.O. Box 690
New York, N.Y. 10019

Please send me the books I have checked. I enclose a check or money order (not cash), plus 50¢ per order and 50¢ per copy to cover postage and handling.*
(Allow 4 weeks for delivery.)

_____ Please send me your free mail order catalog. (If ordering only the catalog, include a large self-addressed, stamped envelope.)

Name _____

Address _____

City _____

State _____ Zip _____

*N.Y. State and California residents add applicable sales tax.

SIZZLING, SIMMERING ROMANTIC ADVENTURE FROM KAREN ROBARDS!

With every new book Karen Robards' fans say, "write us another!"—as thrilling, as passion-filled, as exciting as the last—and she does!

___AMANDA ROSE   (D30-617, $3.50)

A tale of passionate rebellion, a romance as turbulent as the sea itself! An impetuous English beauty, Lady Amanda Rose was determined to escape the loveless marriage her step-brother planned for her. But she was not prepared for the tempestuous love of a pirate that would rob her of her innocence and make her his forever. ...

___TO LOVE A MAN   (D32-605, $3.50, U.S.A.)
                                                  (D30-851, $4.50, Canada)

Lisa Collins is a beautiful, willful, spoiled young woman, recovering from a tragic marriage, now in Africa as a journalist. She is rescued from a terrorist attack by Sam Eastman, a hardened soldier of fortune fighting in Rhodesia's civil war. She wants his help getting home; he wants first to finish the job he was hired for. Out of this conflict and their mutual attraction, comes a raging passion—and one of the hottest contemporary romances you'll ever read.

WARNER BOOKS
P.O. Box 690
New York, N.Y. 10019

Please send me the books I have checked. I enclose a check or money order (not cash), plus 50¢ per order and 50¢ per copy to cover postage and handling.* (Allow 4 weeks for delivery.)

_____ Please send me your free mail order catalog. (If ordering only the catalog, include a large self-addressed, stamped envelope.)

Name _____

Address _____

City _____

State _____ Zip _____

*N.Y. State and California residents add applicable sales tax.   118

There's an epidemic with 27 million victims. And no visible symptoms.

It's an epidemic of people who can't read.

Believe it or not, 27 million Americans are functionally illiterate, about one adult in five.

The solution to this problem is you...when you join the fight against illiteracy. So call the Coalition for Literacy at toll-free **1-800-228-8813** and volunteer.

Volunteer Against Illiteracy. The only degree you need is a degree of caring.

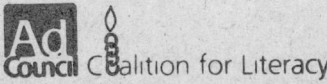

Ad Council — Coalition for Literacy

Warner Books is proud to be an active supporter of the Coalition for Literacy.